And Not Forgetting Love

12 short stories about love,
mistakes and memories

Jenny Roman

ISBN: 978-1-8381832-1-9

DEDICATION

This book is for lovers of the short story, and for those who know that a story about love, just like love itself, may take many forms.

This paperback edition is for readers who still love the feel of the printed page.

CONTENTS

Introduction 1

Symptoms 3

Forgetting 10

Resolution 12

Party Pooper 19

All in the Cards 25

The Middle Drawer 37

Raspberry Ripple 44

Going Solo 51

Skin Deep 56

Luck of the Draw 62

The One Before 85

The Busy Bee 91

About the Stories 98

Bonus story: Five Per Cent 100

About the Author 109

INTRODUCTION

These stories are all about love in its various forms - falling in it, and falling out of it - but they are not necessarily romances. They explore the mistakes we make, situations we run from, misunderstandings we perpetuate, and hidden truths revealed. They include moments of self-delusion, self-denial, forgetting who we are, and remembering who we used to be – all the stuff which makes us human.

For those interested, at the end of the collection there are some additional notes about each story, including details about previous publication (where relevant).

I hope you enjoy this collection, but whatever you think, I'd love to hear your reaction - please consider leaving a review (honestly, it means so much). If you loathed a story, please tell me why. And if you loved one, please tell absolutely *everybody*!

SYMPTOMS

Out of some kind of perverse curiosity, I put my symptoms through one of those on-line medical checkers. I tick headache, lack of appetite, nausea, irregular and racing heartbeat, dizziness, mood swings, sleeplessness, and inability to maintain concentration. My laptop's little blue cursor wheel spins for a few seconds as the website considers my responses, then a list of potential maladies appears. It suggests in particular that I may be suffering from hyperthyroidism, various forms of Cancer, Addison's Disease, a Pulmonary Embolism, or indeed heart failure.

Of course, it's always possible that one or more of these nasties is waiting in the shadows for me, but right now I know the symptom tracker is way off the mark. Hardly surprising - after all, it doesn't know the full story. There isn't a box to tick for "I've met someone, and can't stop thinking about him." If there were such a box, I'm sure it would immediately discount all the other possibilities and present me with only one possible diagnosis: Madam, you appear to have fallen in love.

"Mum?" says a voice behind me.

I slam shut my laptop and swing around guiltily.

Livy is standing in the doorway. Her eyes narrow.

"What's up sweetheart?" I say, my voice sounding falsely bright.

"What are you doing?" she asks.

"Nothing." I stand up, stretch and yawn, like someone who doesn't have a care in the world. "You hungry? Shall I start tea?"

"No, I'm going to Katie's tonight, aren't I? Or did you forget?"

"Oh, silly me. No, of course I'd not forgotten." I feel a twinge of relief: an evening in alone, without having to put on a face. "Have you got your bag packed?"

"Hmm."

"Taking a DVD?"

Livy rolls her eyes at me. "No, we don't need DVDs anymore, mum - we stream all the movies we want to see on Katie's telly."

"Ah yes, she's got that internet do-da, hasn't she."

Livy sighs theatrically. "Mum, you can't really pretend you don't understand it all."

"I'm not pretending, I assure you!"

"You must be. Dad knew how to do all that sort of stuff, and he was much older than you." She stops short; colours a little.

I shrug, to indicate I'm fine with her mentioning Jeff in that casual way. "Your dad was a gadget person. I'm not. Sorry, sweetheart." I rub my hand over my face.

"You look knackered, mum." Livy's voice has altered. There is concern in her eyes. "Maybe I shouldn't go out tonight. Maybe I should stay in with you."

I see my evening alone sliding away. "No, don't be silly. I'm just a bit tired, that's all." I give her another bright smile.

The doorbell chimes and we head down the stairs, Livy dragging her bag behind her. Katie is on the doorstep; her mum waves from the car which is parked, engine running, half on the pavement outside.

"Just a sec - forgotten something," says Livy, and runs

back upstairs. I hold a shouted conversation with Katie's mum across the front garden. When I glance behind me, Livy is coming down again, eyes focused on her feet. Behind her, my study door swings slightly.

"Have fun," I say, and she gives me a fierce hug before she and Katie jump in the car, a mix of banging doors and waving, and then they are gone.

In the quiet that follows, all I hear is my heart beat.

While I defrost a portion of bolognese, I consider my folly. It's not as if I'm a teenager; I'm the wrong side of 40. I've fallen in love before. I should be able to deal with this - should be able to apply maturity and common sense to the situation. I should not be googling my symptoms. Next I'll be practising my signature with his surname.

Ben works on the same floor as me, though in a different department. We did that thing where you bump into each other going to the photocopier or the coffee machine a zillion times, so you feel like you know one another, but then it's embarrassing to admit you don't know each other's names. I had to find out through a casual question in conversation with a colleague - but it obviously wasn't that casual as immediately she grinned and said, "Ah, Ben....nice guy. Divorced a couple of years ago," and winked at me.

Our "courtship" such as it is, has moved painfully slowly. A shared table in the canteen over lunch. A lift home, collecting Livy on the way, when my car had to go to the garage and we realised Ben lived only down the road from us. A lingering conversation following a staff meeting (where we both completely forgot the time and returned to our separate desks long after everyone else, burning with embarrassment). Love has crept up on me. After Jeff died, I didn't expect to meet anyone else, didn't want to. Jeff had been my rock. Yes, he was older than me, but you wouldn't have known it - he was fit and healthy (or so we'd thought), youthful in every way that mattered. The period after his death was a black hole; I could think of nothing but the loss of him. Livy was the only thing which kept me sane during this time; the only person whose suffering equalled my own.

I'm straining the spaghetti when my phone bleeps. I expect it to be Livy (for whom messages are habitual - a constant stream of photos, silly comments, or forgotten-though-now-extremely-important reminders), but it's Ben, and my heart does an adolescent skip. He's had my number since my initial car trouble - though the car has never played up since - and our sporadic texts have always been as shy and careful as we are with each other in person.

- Did you spot Casablanca is on telly tonight? x

I note the kiss. But everyone puts a kiss at the end of texts, don't they? Probably didn't even notice himself doing it.

I tip the spaghetti and the microwave-heated bolognese onto a plate, take it through to the lounge and sit, waiting for my nerve endings to stop fizzing, and my appetite to return. I remember being like this as a teenager, the weight dropping off me as I mooned around over some silly lad or other. Things evidently haven't moved on.

I make myself eat a few mouthfuls, staring blankly at whatever happens to be on the telly, then I put down the plate and text back.

- Ooh, no, hadn't spotted this. Thank you! And thank you for remembering it's my favourite! X

The kiss comes up as a capital letter. Should I change it? Does a big kiss look weird? Then I tell myself to get a grip, and add a second small kiss next to the big one.

- Xx

Yes, that's looks better. Jolly and casual. I press "send" before I can convince myself otherwise.

I busy myself in the kitchen, tip away my largely uneaten dinner, wash up, make myself a mug of tea. Back in the lounge, my phone pings.

- Thought of you straight away when I saw it - can imagine you and Livy having girlie night in. Xx

- Ha! Home alone tonight. (Livy over at a friend's.) What about you? Xx

- Nothing planned. Thinking I'll watch the film - seeing as it comes highly recommended. Xx

I take a deep breath, fingers poised over the screen. Should I? Jeff grins at me from a photo on the side table. He always said you should live life to the full, take every opportunity offered. I blow him a kiss, then look back down at my phone and type:

- Want to watch it over here with me? Promise, no spoilers! Xx

Ben says he'll be about half an hour. I whizz from room to room, plucking our discarded belongings from various places and dumping them back in our respective bedrooms. I spot dust on surfaces which I had hitherto been happy to ignore, and light a scented candle to mask the smell of bolognese. A few minutes later I blow it out, worrying it'll seem like I'm trying too hard. I'm frantically waving my arms around trying to disburse the lingering smell of smoke when the doorbell chimes.

"Didn't want to turn up empty-handed," he says, holding out a bottle of wine, a bag of tortilla chips, and some dip.

On cue, my stomach, which has decided it's now hungry after all, gives an enormous rumble.

"Good job too!" he says, and we both burst out laughing.

And suddenly I know it's going to be fine. We laugh again when he walks into the hall, sniffs and says, "Is something burning?" We grin at each other over glasses of wine. Our hands bump reaching for dip. We watch the film, without really watching the film.

His kiss at the end of the evening is soft, but definite. Like a bookmark. It says we're pausing here, but we are to resume. And the certainty sends a glorious shiver down my spine.

"Will you tell Livy?" he says, standing in the doorway, holding me.

"About the evening?" I ask, grinning, "Or the kiss?"

He dips his head towards me. "About us."

"Yes."

"Good." He smiles. "I don't want to be a nasty surprise."

As if! I had thought, going to bed, head spinning with wine and happiness. But now, leaning against the kitchen cabinets and gazing out of the window, I find myself chewing a nail in agitation. Livy is climbing out of Katie's mum's car, pausing to say her thank-yous, then turning towards the house. My heart is pounding, and my palms feel damp.

"Hey!" she says as we meet in the hall. She hugs me, then pulls away. "You're burning up, mum. Are you OK?"

"Yes, fine, sweetheart. Did you have a good time?"

"You don't look fine. There is something wrong, isn't there? Tell me. Tell me now."

"Oh, look," I sigh. "Just come and sit down for the moment, I do need to tell you something."

"I knew it!" she says.

Sitting at the kitchen table, she bridges her hands, knuckles clenched white. This isn't quite the relaxed and informal way I'd imagined telling her.

"There's really nothing to worry about - but there is something you ought to know."

She won't look me in the eye. She says, speaking to the table, "I already know."

"You know?" I frown at her.

"Yes. I worked it out. You've been acting really weird, you're really tired, and quiet, and when I ask you something it's like you haven't even realised I've spoken. And you've lost weight and you forget stuff all the time.

So, yeah, I pretty much worked it out."

"But how? You've only met Ben a couple of times."

"Ben?" It's Livy's turn to frown. "You mean, it's Ben who's sick?"

"What? No! No-one's sick. What are you talking about?"

"What I've just been saying. All those symptoms - and then you were on that website yesterday, looking up what you had. I saw....I know I shouldn't have looked but..."

My cheeks flush. "That was just me being silly. Yes, I typed in some symptoms, but they were...." I reach across and take her hand. "I've fallen in love."

"With Ben?"

"Yes, with Ben. And I wanted to tell you. We both did. He's in no way trying to replace your dad, or..."

"You actually googled your love symptoms...?" Livy looks at me in disbelief, then comes and throws her arms around me. "I thought you had something awful. I thought I was going to lose you too." She buries her head in my shoulder and squeezes so tight that for a moment I can't breathe.

"Sorry, I didn't think."

Livy looks up. "That's because you're in love. We'd better warn Ben - you're a chronic case!"

FORGETTING

Yesterday, I caught myself putting the teapot in the fridge. It's not the first time I've found myself exhibiting worrying symptoms of my advancing years. Last week, I returned from town empty handed. I'd forgotten my list and simply couldn't remember what I'd gone for. And then there are the usual trivial things; not being able to remember names or what one did yesterday. At moments like this, I imagine you watching me with a half-smile, shaking your head in disbelief. All those jokes we made about old age finally coming true.

Memory is a funny thing. I find my mind clogged with useless information – the registration numbers of cars no longer owned, addresses no longer lived at. Yet the most important details, the exact tone of your voice, the crinkles around your eyes when you were amused by something, what it felt like to press my face against your shoulder in an embrace – these things are sliding away from me, becoming nebulous and ghostly. Of course, I have memories of you. Of course, I know that in your arms I was complete and whole, but I can't remember what that feels like.

They say time is a great healer. And they are right. It

took a long while, but the pain of losing you has begun to lessen. I still miss you (Miss! What an inadequate word for the abyss that remains in my life!) but I can at last go about my everyday business without the perpetual crushing burden of loss. My every waking second is not made agony by your absence.

But I think I would trade, given the choice. I would have back some of the pain if along with it I could truly remember the smell of your skin, the expression in your eyes when they rested on me, the sound of your laugh. If healing is simply forgetting, then I don't want it.

Forgetting sounds careless, as though I've merely misplaced my memories of you by somehow not working hard enough to remember them. I feel as though I didn't concentrate enough when you were here with me, and now I am paying the price. I should have tried harder to fix your image in my mind, to capture the details of your vowel sounds, the feel of your heartbeat, the fragrance of your hair. But of course, being with you was so easy, I never considered the need.

Forgetfulness makes a mockery of all that once seemed so important. All our hopes and fears, all the worries and all the joys which seemed so enormous at the time, slowly eroded by the passing years. Who now sees those castles in the air which we built together?

But one can't dwell on such thoughts. There lies madness, and I am already advancing down that path more swiftly that I care to believe. I will keep going, with stiff-upper-lipped Britishness. I'll start by making tea.

Now, where did I put the teapot?

RESOLUTION

There was paint in her hair. A glob of Cadmium Yellow from where she'd paused to hook a strand behind her ear. The canvas took up almost the whole of one wall of her studio, but she was working in only one corner, close up against the thick texture of the paint, brushstrokes full of a wild energy. When critics talked about her work, they used words like 'abandonment' and 'vitality', said she broke all the rules.

She didn't agree about the last part. Her adherence to rules was precise, but they just couldn't see it. Appreciation of art was not simply about staring at a painting. It was about context, perspective and viewpoint.

*

He'd memorised the route, though the online map had neglected to mention the grimness of the area. From the railway station, he used the pedestrian crossing, then turned right, walking alongside stop-start traffic, fumes rising like dry-ice. By a skanky pub, windows covered over with graffiti-sprayed boards, he turned left, stepping carefully along the edge of a narrow pavement, past the bins, and the dog mess, and the broken bottles. The road ducked down by a disused church, and he passed hard-

edged flats with forbidding railings, knocked about
Edwardian terraces with ugly new porches, and cars
parked on tarmacked front gardens.

The pavement broadened, and the road began to rise
again. The houses were larger, the cars parked on proper
drives. The rumble of traffic grew louder, and he reached a
junction with another main road. He waited for a gap then
darted across. Behind him, he heard the hoot of a horn.

*

Working up close like this, the colours of the canvas
glowed in her peripheral vision, oranges and pinks, so
warm she could almost feel the heat on her face. She was
immersed in colour; like white noise, blocking out
everything else. Under her fingertips, the brush moved
almost of its own accord, dancing over the canvas. She felt
the glow inside of her. *I love this.* It was like flying.

A noise penetrated the hum of her creation. She
paused, the brush stilled in her hand, and cocked her head.
How long had the doorbell been ringing?

*

There was paint in her hair. And on the first two fingers of
her right hand. Yellow paint, so that she looked as if she
was a heavy smoker. She clutched the front door, and did
not step back in invitation, so that he felt disadvantaged on
the bottom step, gazing up.

"This is my New Year's resolution!"

He'd got it all prepared, his little speech. Had imagined
all kinds of reactions, but her stillness unnerved him, so he
got no further.

"It's April," she said, flatly.

He shrugged. "Timing was never my strong point."

She stared. The silence lengthened between them. The
seconds stretched out agonisingly. He dropped his gaze.
Swallowed. Heard the blood singing in his ears.

"Sorry. Stupid of me," he said. He felt defeated. Had
worked himself up to this over weeks and weeks. Had not
slept the previous night, but tossed and turned, sweaty in

his bed. Now he was washed out. Exhausted.

"No," she said. "Surprising. Not stupid."

*

The front room was a tip. She bundled up some unopened mail, newspapers, an old jumper, so he could sit down on the sagging sofa, but there was no embarrassment in her briskness. You turned up unannounced, she seemed to say, take me as you find me.

She went through a narrow door to a kitchen at the back, and he heard sounds of the kettle going on, the chink of a spoon against a mug. He sat with his knees poking up to the ceiling, paralysed by self-doubt, and waited for her.

*

While the kettle boiled, she stood by the back door, staring out blankly at the yard. It had rained overnight so that the wooden fence was dark with moisture, the paving slabs dull grey. There was no colour.

In the glass, her reflection stared back at her. She shivered. She didn't know why he'd come. Not now, after all this time. What was there to say?

*

"Sorry, it's black. There's no milk." She held out a mug towards him, and was careful that their fingers didn't touch as he took it.

"It's fine," he said, though it wasn't really. He sipped the coffee, bitter and too hot.

Another silence. Other people he knew would have made conversation, broken the ice. But she simply waited for him. He was the one who'd decided to come, after all.

"How've you been?" he asked at length.

"Fine." She shrugged. "Good."

"You've got an exhibition I hear?"

She nodded. "In two weeks. It's in a converted warehouse. So people can stand back to view the paintings. They don't really work in a gallery."

He nodded, pretending he knew what she meant.

"And you?"

"Oh…you know." He couldn't begin. His life was an empty crater. He got up, went to work, shopped for food, maintained the flat, did his laundry, filled up the car with petrol, watched telly, slept.

He stared at the pattern in the carpet, frowning. It couldn't have been her choice. It was hideous. When they'd lived together, he'd always felt he'd been a block to her self-expression. He'd expected her own place to be tastefully, if eccentrically, decorated, filled with beautiful objects. A physical reflection of her artistic mind. But the house was ordinarily shabby, disappointing.

*

She didn't sit down, but parked herself against the windowsill, arms folded across her chest. She wasn't trying to shut him out, but hold herself in.

He'd aged. Of course. His face was more drawn, his hair a little thinner. There seemed to be altogether less of him.

"So, why was this your New Year's Resolution?" she asked.

He gazed up at her. "Because I've never stopped thinking about you."

She sighed.

"I don't expect you to say the same," he said quickly. "I know I'm easily forgotten.'

"Don't."

"I'm not having a go. Honestly. I didn't come here to make you feel bad. I just made a promise to myself, that I'd come and see you. That's all." He forced a grin. "I'd kind of hoped you'd got really fat and old, but no such luck."

She made a face.

"Could I see something you're working on?" he asked. "In case I don't make the exhibition?"

She gazed upwards for a moment, as though trying to see through the floorboards to the studio above. She hated taking people up there. Showing people work which wasn't quite finished. A chef wouldn't invite someone to taste a dish before it was cooked. But she found herself saying, "Yeah, course."

She pushed herself away from the windowsill and led him up the creaking staircase to the studio which stretched across the back of the house. She tried to see the canvas in the way he would see it – for the first time, with no idea of what it meant. A cacophony of colour.

His eyes darted over the painting, and she saw him frown.

"It doesn't work in here," she said quickly, "you'd need to stand much further back to get the effect."

"What effect?"

"It'll look beautiful. Difficult to believe, I know, but it will."

"What's it supposed to be exactly?" He gave a self-deprecating laugh to indicate that his lack of interpretation was a failing on his part, not the fault of the painting.

She ran her hands through her hair. "OK. You know when they send back pictures from space, and the earth is this beautiful blue green swirling globe? It looks perfect?"

He nodded.

"Or when you're flying, and you look down on a city and it looks amazing. But you know that in reality, down on the ground, there's all kinds of ugliness – run-down buildings, landfill sites, people doing awful things to one another. When you look at something from a distance, you don't see the gory details. That's what this painting is about – you look at it here, up close, and there's chaos, and clashes of colour, and ugliness. But when you stand back in the exhibition hall, it'll look beautiful."

"But you painted it in here?"

She nodded.

"So how do you know?"

She shrugged. "I just know."

*

They went back downstairs to the scruffy lounge. The weight of his visit hung over them once more. He tried to focus, to remember the point of it all, a nebulous idea of what Americans called 'closure'.

From his pocket, he withdrew something wrapped in tissue paper. He held it out to her and she took it uncertainly.

"I want you to have it back," he said.

She unwrapped the package. In a tiny frame sat an exquisitely painted miniature; a tree, the fine detail breathtaking, and in the trunk of the tree, their initials, as if carved. Forever.

"Do you remember painting that?" he asked.

She nodded.

"You said the tree was us. You can't see the deep roots in the picture, but you know they're there, holding up the tree – you said that was how it was with us."

She nodded, miserably.

"Afterwards, I thought it was funny," he went on. "Turned out we didn't have any roots at all."

"Please…" she said.

"Sorry. I didn't mean… I wanted you to have it back, to remember the kind of artist you used to be. The kind of person you used to be."

She said nothing, but he saw moisture glittering in her eyes.

"Anyway, that was all," he said. He was aware a weight had shifted. He smiled at her. "Thanks for the coffee."

He went towards the front door to let himself out. She didn't move.

*

The sun had come out. His skin reached out towards the light and heat. He walked quickly, the blood pumping round his body, the energy flowing through him. He'd done it. He'd bloody done it.

The world had been brought into high definition. Branches of trees, edges of buildings stood out sharply against the sky. He walked back to the station and the world was alive around him. This time he didn't notice the dog mess, or the broken bottles, or the graffiti.

*

There was paint in her hair. She stood in front of the mirror with the miniature in her hands, looking from her reflection to the image and back. He was right. She wouldn't have been able to paint such a thing now. She was a different artist, and a different person.

She looked at the painting, and then at the crumpled tissue paper, and then at her own hands. She'd never noticed before how lined they had become. Skin mottled, dirty paint ingrained in the creases and wrinkles. Cadmium Yellow.

PARTY POOPER

My shoes feel stiff and tight, and the little toe of my right foot is rubbing painfully even sitting in the upright wooden chairs of the waiting room. It was stupid to wear heels. What am I trying to prove? That I am somehow more credible because I have posh shoes?

I imagine Nick attending a similar appointment across town somewhere. Would he have dressed up? Hardly. "Take me as they find me!" he'd say. The thought of him makes my heart tip over. I've not seen him for eight days. He's been kipping at Pete's since he moved out.

I glance at my watch again. I've been here 27 minutes. Granted, I arrived early, sticky with apprehension, but even so, they've kept me waiting. The receptionist has offered no explanation nor, for that matter, so much as acknowledged my existence following her curt request that I take a seat. I am too cowardly to enquire about the delay.

This wouldn't happen to Nick. He'd have engaged the prickly woman in conversation by now - would have had her laughing and joking. She'd probably have made him a cuppa.

I watch as she deals briskly and efficiently with various telephone calls, taps away at her keyboard, files a document in a ring binder with a satisfying click, and sends something to her desktop printer. She is not in the least bit fazed by my being there. I know that if our roles were reversed, I would be all fingers and thumbs, bumbling under scrutiny.

A door to my left opens suddenly, and a small, fine woman appears, with close cropped hair, and a suit so sharp it can only have been tailor made. She stares at me piercingly through narrow rimmed glasses and says, "Ms Sanderson?"

It is probably my imagination, but I feel sure she has deliberately stressed the 'Ms'. I want to correct her and say, "Mrs" but of course this is precisely why I'm here.

I push myself out of the unforgiving chair, get awkwardly to my feet (my little toe protesting as I do so) and I hold out my hand. She gives me a dead fish handshake. This would be the natural moment for her to apologise for keeping me waiting, but she doesn't. Instead she says, "Marion Richards" as though I might be in any doubt.

I follow her into an office which seems to be an extension of her own persona – small, but expensively furnished, and not a blunt pencil, chewed biro, or dog-eared document to be seen. I try and fail to imagine what it must be like to be so uber-organised.

She indicates for me to take a seat, and steps precisely around her desk, picking up a file before seating herself. I notice Sanderson v Sanderson on a neatly typed label. A leaden weight settles in my stomach.

"Now then, there are a number of issues we need to address in the Acknowledgement of Service."

"I'm sorry, the what?"

She gives me a long-suffering glance. "There was a comprehensive breakdown of all the relevant stages in the paperwork I sent you on -" She pauses to flick briefly and precisely through a series of documents, "the seventeenth. You received this, yes?"

It's like being back at school, having failed to submit a piece of homework on time. I nod, and feel compelled to add, "But I've not had much of a chance to -"

"This process is much more straightforward if you can take the time to familiarise yourself with the key procedures before you come into the office." She stares somewhere over my right shoulder. "Mr Sanderson has submitted the divorce petition, and thus we must now submit the Acknowledgement of Service – that is, whether or not you intend to contest the divorce or allow it to proceed."

I feel a rising bubble of hysteria building within me. *Allow it to proceed.* As if the power was mine. As if I could, of my own choosing, stop this lumbering wreck of a marriage from plunging downhill, gathering momentum as the minutes fly by, heading inexorably to the immense stone wall of divorce. Boom.

I swallow noisily, scared I might actually laugh - or worse, cry. Marion Richards stares at me with barely suppressed disdain. She raises her eyebrows and inclines her head as though expecting a response. I'm not sure if she's actually asked me a question.

"I...I don't know. I mean, none of this is my decision. I was quite happy...." I stumble to a halt, knowing this last isn't quite true. I can't remember when I was last happy.

She sighs, as though I'm being rather tiresome, and then says, "So you want to contest?" She starts to tap something briskly into her computer. "And on what grounds?"

"We can't get divorced," I blurt. "I still love him."

Her hands go still on the keyboard, but she doesn't look at me. "I'm afraid that's irrelevant right now."

Of all the things that possibly could be relevant in this precise situation, surely this is the most important? I want to say this to her - or rather, to shout it out, jumping up and slamming the table. *I love him. I love him. We can't be getting divorced!* But of course, I don't. I sit there, mute.

Sensible and self-contained.

Her lips narrow, and then she says, "We need to address, in turn, each of the issues raised by the party of the first part."

"Party?" Unbidden, an image flies into my mind of Nick at a friend's birthday party years ago, throwing himself around the floor to the tune of 'Dancing Queen' while the rest of us clutch our sides laughing.

"Mr Sanderson." She gives a long suffering sigh. "Mr Sanderson is the party of the first part. You are the party of the second part."

I imagine us in court - the party of the first part: *the Party Animal*, and the party of the second part: *the Party Pooper!* Nick would be radiating joy and fun, while I would stand there rigid and aloof. The image is like a photograph in my mind.

I can guess the kind of things that will have been cited by Nick as grounds for my "unreasonable behaviour". Have I ever strayed into the arms of another? No. Have I stayed out partying until the wee small hours? No. Have I constantly spent the housekeeping on new clothes? No. Perhaps it would have been better if I had! In doing none of those things, I have, in fact, simply fallen into the habit of drudgery, of doing - and being - nothing at all.

Something inside me snaps. I stand up so quickly that the chair rocks back slightly before coming to rest against the backs of my knees. The blood rushes from my head; I feel dizzy with the impossibility of it all.

"Nick," I say.

"I'm sorry?" She does actually look startled.

"Nick. His name is Nick. He isn't a *party*, he is a person. A wonderful, warm, bright, fantastic person. And an amazing husband." I grab my bag. "And we are not getting divorced."

In my stupid heels, I flee Marion Richards' office, stumbling past the receptionist and out into the corridor.

It's so clear now, what has happened to us. The more

irresponsible Nick acts, the more cautious I am in response. The more sensible I become, the more frivolous Nick feels he needs to be. I go to work, I earn a living, I keep the house - even though Nick demands none of this from me and would, in fact, probably prefer it if I said I wanted to jack in my job, sell the house and go InterRailing for three years! The girl he married - the daft, young thing who didn't have a penny to her name and didn't care - disappeared years ago, eroded by responsibility. The woman who replaced her, sensible, pragmatic, reserved, has driven him away.

I tumble out of the office door, into the street, blinking as though seeing the world for the first time. Everything is sharply defined, the colours more vivid, the light brighter. My ankle twists painfully in my posh shoes, and I put a hand out to steady myself against the wall.

The memory of that party lingers in my mind, as if it were instead a film made about two other, brighter, better people. We'd had so many dreams, so much energy and determination. We weren't going to be like everyone else. And yet here we are - falling apart because we've devoted too much time to paying the mortgage for a house Nick can no-longer bear to call his home.

What happened to fun? Nick has done his best to keep the joy in our relationship, but I've seen all his attempts as childish, pointless. I've been the damper on his every suggestion, all his plans and schemes. Mrs Negative. Mrs Cautious. Mrs Gloom.

I kick my shoes off and start to run in my stockinged feet, dangling the shoes from one hand, my bag from the other. I attract glances from passers-by. Silly middle-aged woman acting like a teenager. But I don't care. I think of us coming back from that party - having missed all the buses and unable to find a taxi. I'd kicked off my shoes back then too - and we'd walked miles, yelping and giggling. The hangover the next day had been awful and I'd vowed never again.

But never is a long time. You can't be sensible all the time. You have to live a little. Nick knows that - it's what he's been trying to get me to do all these years.

I speed up, dodging other pedestrians on the pavement. I hope it's not too late.

And then I see a man walking along the pavement towards me from one of the side-streets, his shoulders hunched, staring at the floor. A man who looks like my Nick, but without the smile.

I come to a sudden halt and drop my shoes. They clatter to the ground, and the sound makes him look up. I see his expression alter; see a moment's incomprehension, and then he's coming towards me, uncertainly. My heart is thudding, and it's only partly because of the running. We meet on the corner and stand together in the middle of the pavement, people tutting and squeezing by us on either side. Even though Nick only left just over a week ago, it is like seeing him anew. We stare at each other for what seems an age, though is probably only a few seconds.

"I've missed you," I tell him.

There is a pause, and I stand on the edge of a yawning chasm expecting to fall.

"Me too." He reaches out a hand, takes hold of my sleeve.

I feel a lump in my throat.

He glances down. "What happened to your shoes?"

I shrug. "I decided they didn't go with my outfit."

He starts to laugh. It's a sound I've not heard in a long time. I begin to laugh too, but there are tears rolling down my cheeks. He puts an arm around my shoulders and pulls me to him. I rest my head against his chest and it feels like it did when we were just getting together, when we didn't know if it was going to work out between us.

We still don't. But standing there in his arms, I think there's a chance.

ALL IN THE CARDS

Karen leant against the sea wall, hands thrust deep into her pockets, and felt the wind sharp on her face. Above, two gulls circled lazily, uttering desolate cries. On the beach below, a couple walked sedately, a small terrier crossing and re-crossing in front of them, vacuuming smells. Farther out, by the water line, a fisherman was crouching over his lines, and in the distance, a lone jogger made tracks in the wet sand.

She felt a prickling sense of unease; *I should be doing something.* The counsellor had suggested she ought to concentrate on absorbing the moment, live in the present, observe the here and now. But, despite the buffeting wind, this sense of stillness was alien and uncomfortable.

Until now, her life had been a continual battle against the clock, from the moment the alarm pierced the silence of her bedroom in the morning, to the end of the day when she climbed gratefully back in under the duvet, head pounding, mind still racing with a hundred and one things she should have done.

So what was she doing back here, loitering on the sea front like an out of season tourist?

In her left pocket, her fingertips curled around the

playing card. She withdrew it, lay it face up on the sea wall and held it steady with carefully manicured fingertips.

The glib answer was that she was here because of the Four of Clubs.

Looking at the card again sent a jolt through her body. The edges were frayed and grubby. Hardly surprising - the pack it had come from was well over twenty years old. She'd been with Matt, the cocky lad from next door, when she'd found the cards in a revolving rack near the ice-cream kiosk. They were just kids then - eleven, twelve at most. In fairness, the playing card idea probably hadn't been a bad marketing strategy. On the face of each card, in the centre, was a different scene depicting the many and varied attractions of the local area. But the execution had been poor; the photographs uninspired, the printing smudged, the colours over-bright.

Matt, flush with newly acquired pocket money from helping his dad on his latest DIY project, had bought a set straightaway, and the two of them made it their mission to visit every place on the cards. The packs became so well used that they began to identify each destination by its corresponding card. They no longer met at the swimming pool, but at the "Nine of Spades", school was the "Jack of Diamonds" and so forth.

A blast of wind hit her so hard she had to brace herself against the sea wall. Her legs were still wobbly. The doctor had warned her not to overdo it. She was supposed to "be kind" to herself - the effects of long-term stress on the body were always difficult to quantify. She hated all that nonsense. She'd coped fine all these years with her demanding lifestyle. Why had it all of a sudden slid away from her so absolutely? But the memory of her last day in the office, the expressions on the faces of her colleagues, the way they would no longer meet her eye, still made her shudder.

And that's when the envelope had turned up on her desk, containing a single playing card - the Four of Clubs, the jetty. She'd found herself agreeing to "gardening leave", throwing some things in a bag, and heading straight here, though she couldn't explain why. Nostalgia?

Coming back felt like an admission of defeat. OK, so she'd lived here briefly after university, but it had never been more than a temporary return. In such a small town, there were few jobs, no real prospects. There was just the security of the familiar, her family and few remaining friends. And Matt of course.

The gulls screeched, and the sound made the years tumble away so that she was 12 again, standing on the sea front in the school holidays, eating chips with her mates, waving at her dad as he drove by in his post van, and knowing her mum would be just about to go on her lunch break from cashiering in the little building society on the corner.

Perhaps if Matt had asked her to stay back then, everything would have been different.

She took a deep breath. For years she'd tried her best not to think of Matt, relegated him to just a figure from her past. She kept herself so focused on work there wasn't time to dwell on what might have been - not in the sprint to the train each morning, in the race from office to meeting, from meeting to client brief, from client brief to corporate lunch. By the time she made it home in the evenings, she was too tired to think of anything much at all.

Now things were different. Standing here, with the scent of the sea air, memories were crowding in. She glanced about her, self-consciously. If this had been a film, right now Matt would be striding towards her, cheesy music playing in the background. But there was just an old lady clutching her shopping bags, one hand determinedly hanging on to her hat, and a guy in his sixties talking loudly into his mobile phone, stray words being snatched away by the wind.

She turned, her hair whipping across her face, and

headed down the concrete steps to the beach. It was a short walk to the stubby jetty. She squinted at the playing card again - there was a tiny "X" inked on in biro over the smudgy photograph. Third strut along. She stepped carefully across the damp sand in her elegant designer boots, and gazed up at the algae-stained concrete. Yes, there was something there! A small brown envelope, wedged into the corner with the upright. She had to stand on tip-toe to reach.

Inside was the Seven of Spades: The Park.

The park had both shrunk and grown. Shrunk in the sense that the housing estates which had sprung up around its boundaries made it no longer a wilderness to explore. Grown in the sense that in the play area, the swings and climbing frames, so much smarter and brighter, were now dwarfed by the wooden adventure playground which had been erected around it. Play was a much more organised business in this day and age, it seemed. Karen tested the spongy rubber flooring beneath the slide - the hard concrete where she'd grazed her knees so many times had long since gone.

There was a stout fence around the duck pond, and an instruction not to feed bread to the ducks - instead, you could feed special duck food available from the kiosk. The kiosk was shut, and there were no ducks in evidence. Perhaps they'd gone to other ponds where forbidden bread was still freely available.

When she and Matt had been kids their favourite thing had been the swings. Even when they were really too old, they'd sit there of an evening, talking and half-heartedly swinging, kicking their trainers into the dusty soil. The new swings were bright and shiny, and there was more rubber flooring. There was no place to hide another envelope.

She felt deflated, and at once irritated. Was this Matt's idea of a joke? Did he now live in one of these new estate houses and was even at this moment watching her standing there like an idiot?

And then it came to her. The hollow oak. Of course, they'd made a den! She drifted towards the edge of the park, where the trees still stood in a thick band before the stout wooden fences of the new gardens. The old oak was now almost hidden from view by the growth of its neighbours. Of course, the den wouldn't still be there, would it? Not after all this time. Feeling slightly self-conscious though there was no-one about, she stepped off the path and slipped into the woodland, ducking under branches and stepping carefully over the soft, leaf-littered ground.

The damp moss smell of the woodland spun her back through time. Forgetting herself, she crouched at the base of the oak, peering into the semi-rotten interior of the hollowed out trunk. It was amazing the tree was still standing, that it hadn't been torn in two by some storm or other in the intervening years, but here it was - looking almost exactly as it had always done. The den itself seemed tiny now. It was difficult to imagine they'd spent so much time in here. Thankfully, the hideous old orange sleeping bag they used to sit on was long gone.

She couldn't scramble all the way into the hollow in her smart trousers and long boots, but she perched on the edge, and leaned in, her fingertips exploring the contours of the tree's inners. The wood was soft and damp, but off to the right, she encountered something cold, hard and angular. Yes, of course! Their keepsakes were always held in an old metal box pushed up into the rotting core of the tree.

I wonder, she thought, reaching gingerly up into the hollow.

The box brought with it a shower of dead insects and slivers of rotten wood. She knocked the worst of the bits from her sleeves and laughed at herself, trying to imagine someone from the office seeing her now.

"Matt, this is ridiculous!" she said out loud. But she

couldn't ignore the shiver of delight down her spine from this treasure hunt of memories.

She prised open the box and felt a flicker of triumph. There was another envelope. She tore it open. The Ten of Diamonds: The Cinema.

The cinema was shut. Not just shut, but by the looks of the outdated film posters fading in their peeling frames, closed down completely. Was this the end of the trail? She felt confused and disappointed, and there was also a pang of regret for the old place where they'd seen so many films over the years. Films and, of course, that first kiss. She felt her cheeks flushing at the memory. So unexpected. They'd been giggling together about something, and then his lips had been on hers, and everything had gone still within her. After so many years of friendship, they'd finally crossed that intangible line.

They had not been able to re-cross it.

They had tried. Kept up the old routines, the same jokes, the same laughs - except the laughter was somehow forced, the grins too wide. They didn't seem to be able to move forward either. There were no more kisses. Karen had assumed she was just a rubbish kisser. Maybe he'd just been curious, and now curiosity was satisfied, and that was that.

Karen cupped her hands against the glass of the main doors and peered in, but the foyer was too gloomy for her to be able to see much at all. She went slowly back down the steps, and round to the left. There was another door, covered with the same peeling paint. To her surprise, it was unlocked. The hinges were stiff, and there was a pile of old leaves wedged up behind it, but she managed to slip through the gap. She found herself in a tiny porch. The inner door into the building itself was locked, and she realised this was the old back exit which would have been used in an emergency or when the building was particularly packed. People from the top rows could come down the back stairs this way.

She was just about to back out, when she saw an old leaflet rack screwed to the wall on the left. She ran her hands over the outdated photos of bygone attractions. That's when she found the envelope.

The Ace of Hearts: The Cherry Tree pub.

It was the right place, of that she was certain, but it looked completely different. When they were kids, it had been the kind of pub people said had 'rustic charm', but was actually a bit twee: cream painted, with flowery curtains and outside, wooden benches and hanging baskets. Now it was a chic sage green, with the window frames picked out in grey, and the door flanked by two neatly clipped bay trees in pots.

Karen put her hand on the sleek satin-finish finger plate, pushed open the door and stepped into the cool, classy interior.

There was the satisfying clink of glass and cutlery from the restaurant area off to the right. Karen couldn't remember when she'd last eaten. There was a hollow empty feeling in her stomach, but she was too on edge to feel hungry. She stepped down a couple of wide flagstone steps into the bar area, and glanced around. A waitress was just disappearing into the kitchen, but there was no-one else in evidence.

Just then she heard a man's voice, part way through a conversation, coming down the stairs behind the bar. It was a voice she'd listened to a thousand times buried in her subconscious. A voice she'd never expected to hear again.

She stood rooted to the spot, not knowing if she wanted to rush headlong into the next moment, or turn and run.

He came striding into the bar with a catering-sized box of crisps in his hands, dropped the box on the bar, and glanced up with a smile to welcome his next punter. The smile faded into something else altogether.

For a moment, neither of them spoke, then Matt said simply, "Thank God."

"I got your message," said Karen, holding up the playing cards in fan. "Most people would have just phoned."

Matt shook his head with a rueful grin. "I didn't have the nerve." He half made a movement to come towards her, then halted. "I can't believe you're actually here."

Karen wondered if she measured up to his mental image of her. How much had she changed?

"Listen, can I get you a drink?" said Matt, recovering himself. "On the house, of course. Wine, or...?"

"Could I just have a coffee? I'm not really drinking at the moment."

"Yes, of course. Have a seat over there in the corner, and I'll be right with you."

Karen made her way self-consciously to the corner booth, legs like jelly. She slid gratefully onto the comfortable padded bench, dropped the fan of playing cards onto the table, and shrugged herself out of her coat. Behind the bar, Matt was busying himself with the coffee machine. She watched his hands, deft at the various levers and knobs. She could hardly believe she was here either. She could feel her pulse throbbing in her neck. What had the doctor said about avoiding stressful situations?

Matt was coming across the flagstone floor towards her, eyes on the tray in his hands. Karen gazed into his face, searching out the boy in the man he had become. He was so painfully still her Matt that the breath felt tight in her lungs. Was she having another panic attack? No. It wasn't that at all.

"Here we are," he said, busying himself with the coffee cups, sachets of sugar, a few biscotti biscuits. He glanced at her, flashed a quick smile, before pulling out a chair to sit opposite her. "Did you want something to eat? I could get..."

She put her hand out, and shook her head. "No, let's just - "

He took a breath, paused. "Sorry... I've imagined this moment a thousand times. But, of course in my imagination, I'm much more cool, and I can think of all the right things to say."

She grinned, and saw him relax a little.

"This place looks amazing, by the way." She gazed around the pub. "You've transformed it."

"Thanks. There's lots more I'd like to do, but it's been a long haul to get this far. Everything costs more and takes more time than you think it will, but I'm getting there."

"How long have you had the pub?"

"This one? Eighteen months. I'd been a tenant in a couple of others, you know, learning the ropes, but this is a free house, so I'm not answerable to anyone else and I can run it the way I want. I'm pretty proud of the old place to be fair."

"So you should be."

There was a pause. Matt stirred his coffee, then glanced up. "So, how are you?" His blue eyes rested on her, searching her face. "I mean, I know... Your mum mentioned to my mum that you'd... not been too good."

And there it was. The small town community jungle drums. Karen waited for the familiar flush of irritation and resentment. How many other people knew about her personal life? This was what she'd hated about living here.

But the feeling wasn't there anymore. And she knew why. Without those jungle drums she wouldn't be here sitting opposite Matt right now.

"I'm...taking some time off. You know, 're-evaluating my work/life balance'." She drew quotation marks in the air.

"Well, that's good. Taking a break and all that." Matt winced. "Sorry, I don't know how to say anything which means anything!" He glanced down at his coffee. "Will you...go back?"

"I don't know. I used to believe I couldn't imagine anything else. Now? I'm not sure there's anything to go back for."

"No pining boyfriend?"

"Nope," said Karen. "I've a very nice flat which would sell in the blink of an eye if I wanted it to. A few so-called friends who've been too embarrassed to ring me and see if I'm ok. I'm not even sure if realistically I have a job to go back to. I mean, they said all the right things at the time, but I'm sure it would be easier all round if I just stepped away quietly."

"And is that what you want?"

"Of course not. I want them to tell me they can't manage without me and beg me to come back!" She gave a little laugh to prove she wasn't quite serious. "Oh, I don't know. It's just a bit of a shock when you've seen yourself as one kind of person for such a long time and then you discover actually deep down you're someone completely different."

"You shouldn't beat yourself up. People change over time. What you wanted as a twenty-something isn't necessarily what you want now. That's not an admission of defeat. It's just life."

He gestured to the playing cards. "Look, sorry about all this. I know it was all ridiculously elaborate. I guess I hoped you might consider coming home, but I wanted to make it easy for you if that wasn't part of your plan. Easy for me too. If you hadn't turned up, I could assume you'd not got the cards, or had just thought it was silly. I could convince myself it wasn't that you didn't want to see me."

"Matt, the trail was amazing."

"Really?"

"Yes. A proper paper chase of all our old haunts!"

"It was a lot of fun to set up. Brought back a lot of memories."

Their eyes met. Karen wondered if they were both thinking about the same memory in particular. The one from the cinema.

"And the trail brought me here to you." Karen gazed around the pub. "Can't believe how much you've done to this place."

"Thanks, that means a lot. Didn't think it would impress a city girl!" Matt leant back in his chair. "It was a slog, I don't mind admitting. But I've got a good team around me now, and I'm getting to the stage where I can afford to step back a little. Make some time for my own life."

Karen paused a beat. "You've been running it on your own then?"

"Yeah, but I've got some really good staff - some who've come with me from the other pubs - so..." Matt paused, and gave a wry smile. "That's not what you're asking me, is it?"

Karen tipped her head in acknowledgement, not quite meeting his eye.

"No, I'm not with anyone at the moment," he said. "There was someone, a while back, but it didn't work out."

"How come?"

"Lots of reasons." He paused. "Mainly because she wasn't you."

Karen felt her heart turn over.

"When I got back from Uni," she said, "why did you never ask me to stay?"

Matt shrugged. "I knew this little town wasn't enough for you. I wanted you to stay because that's what you wanted too. Back then if you'd stayed for me, you'd have ended up resenting me, and I couldn't have lived with that."

Karen took a sip of her coffee. "What's that quote about travelling the world in search of what you need and coming home to find it?" She put down the cup, looked up and met Matt's blue, blue eyes. "So, I followed the paper trail. I got all the clues. Isn't it time you let me know the prize?"

Matt gave a rueful laugh. "I'm afraid there's no prize - you just get left with The Joker."

She pushed the playing cards towards him. "D'you think it's about time we stopped playing games and laid all our cards on the table?"

Matt rolled his eyes. "How long have you been working on that terrible gag?" He reached forwards, put his hand over hers, and squeezed her fingers in his own.

And that's when she knew her decision was made: she was coming home.

THE MIDDLE DRAWER

It feels like the fabric of the flat is shaking. My heartbeat echoes the thumping at the door. In the dark, I grope for Leo, but of course he's not there. I swing myself out of bed, grab my dressing gown, pad down the carpeted hall to the front door. I wish for Leo's big comforting bulk, for him to be able to deal with whatever this is.

"Alright!" I shout, as the banging starts up again.

Jason from the flat upstairs is standing there in his boxers and a sleep-creased t-shirt. His feet are wet. A trail of damp footprints runs from the communal stairs.

"Sorry Frances," he says, "Nat left the bloody bath running and then fell asleep. There's a tidal-wave in our hall – must have come through your ceiling by now."

I look round in the direction of our own bathroom, expecting to see water seeping from the ceiling, but nothing appears wrong.

"Not that side," says Jason following my gaze, "Our bathroom's over here." He waves his hand to the room on the other side of the hall, pushes by me and tries to open the door.

"It's locked!"

"Leo's study. He always keeps it locked."

"Got the key?"

"Yes, but I'm not-" I stop. How can I say I'm not allowed to open it? This is the twenty-first century; I'm Leo's wife. "He doesn't like people going in there," I finish lamely.

"Yeah, and he won't like it when all his sodding novels are papier-mâché either. Get the flaming key!"

His logic is irrefutable. I fetch the key from the peg in the kitchen, the fob pristine and unworn. Leo, of course, has his own.

As I slide the key into the lock I tell myself it's an emergency. It's not as if I'll touch anything unless it's absolutely necessary. But my hand fumbles the simple task.

"Never," he said when I first moved in, "never go in there."

I laughed. And then something in his expression stopped me short. His eyes, which normally rested on me with benign good humour, were black and glittering. My hands went up in a gesture of submission. "Okay. Of course I won't." Almost instantly his easy smile was back in place, the crinkles round his eyes assuring me that all was well, the moment had passed. But a tiny chill settled over me, as though the thermostat of our relationship had been turned down just a degree.

Even as Jason barks, "Don't!" I've clicked the light switch. There is an instant of brightness, before everything goes off. The whole flat is plunged into darkness.

"That's the electric buggered," says Jason, with a trace of satisfaction. I have lived up to his low expectations of me.

"No, it'll be the trip." I push the light switch back to the off position, and then feel my way down the hall to the kitchen. As my eyes adjust, there is enough artificial light from outside for me to pull out a chair, stand on it, flick the trip switch. The hall light comes back on.

We peer into the study to confirm what we both know we've already seen, like a subliminal message, in the split second of light.

A bare box. A ghostly glow is reflected from the white painted walls. To the right, there are four utilitarian shelves attached to the wall by brackets. Empty. To the left, a wire mesh style office bin containing a single piece of screwed up paper, like the recycle bin icon on a computer. Along the back wall, there's a plain white desk, with three drawers to the left hand side. The only items on the desk are a laptop and a printer. No pens, pencils, notebooks, pieces of paper, no mugs, letters, envelopes, books. Nothing.

The ceiling bows in an impossible curve, the water a malignant force pushing at the plaster.

"Better get everything out before it goes." Jason strides in, starts unplugging the laptop and printer, pulling the cabling free of the desk legs. "Thought there'd be more stuff in here – good job, huh?"

"Hmm."

I watch Jason's deft movements, transfixed, as though it is his home, not mine. Then I make myself go in. I hesitate, expecting…what? To be struck down by some mighty force? Leo to appear, shouting at me? Nothing happens. Of course nothing happens. Jason carries out the printer and laptop. I go through the drawers. I want them to be full of stuff. I want Leo to have swept his hand across the stationery detritus which littered the desk as he worked, and shoved everything into the drawers. I want that to explain the starkness of his supposedly creative space.

The top drawer contains one spiral bound reporter's notebook, apparently unused. And a black biro. My stomach muscles spasm. In the middle drawer, there's a large battered envelope, which obviously contains a manuscript. I take it and shut the drawer. The bottom drawer is deep, and contains hanging files. I flick through each quickly. Empty.

My guts twinge again.

"That all?" Jason glances at the envelope in my hands.

I nod.

"Then let's get out. Ceiling could go any sec."

I fetch old towels and spread them on the floor in the hope of catching the worst of it when it finally goes. We stand in the hall waiting for the crash.

"What was Nat doing running the bath in the middle of the night?" I ask, an attempt to divert myself from the black hole in my mind.

"On shifts, isn't she? Dunno what she was thinking though. Idiot." He glances around the flat. "Where's Leo this time?"

"Manchester. Talking to MA students about the book."

Leo's talk has barely changed since I heard it the first time as a wide-eyed student myself. He is a good orator and funny with it – a fact which has allowed him to keep touring the circuit despite having only that one novel to his name. Holding the audience in the palm of his hand, he keeps a careful balance between self-deprecation – astounded at his own success – and the self-assurance which comes with his position. The most riveting part is when he talks about how the writing process takes over, absorbs you, fills you up so there's no space for other thoughts, feelings, desires. At this point, he assumes an expression not unlike someone undergoing some kind of spiritual enlightenment (often mirrored in the upturned faces of his audience). He says, "It's as though another hand, not your own, is forcing you to put the words on the page."

Jason sniffs. "He wants to stop talking about that book and get on with writing another one!"

We hear water dripping steadily onto the surface of the desk.

Jason rolls his eyes. "Sorry, Frances. I'll get onto the insurers first thing."

It's starting to get light. Pointless to go back to bed, I put the kettle on, sit at the kitchen table with a cup of tea in my lap and stare at the envelope.

Leo always jokes that when we met he fleeced me for a quid – he the famous writer, me the penniless student. Like most of his stories, it's a mild distortion of the truth. He didn't have any change for the coffee machine. I gave him two fifty pence pieces.

As he fed my money into the machine, he said, "You were at the book signing just now."

"That's right," I said, embarrassed and pleased that he'd recognised me.

Afterwards, I felt a fool because I realised he'd just noticed the copy of his book in my bag, nestled up against my notebook where I kept all my own meagre jottings and scribbles.

He took my name and number – said he had to pay me back – but I never expected him to call.

Of course, I knew all about Tara, his first wife. Everyone knew. About her mental health problems; how after she'd died, he'd written *The Knife Edge* - telling her story. He'd been an overnight success, from small press obscurity straight into the best seller listings, the book seen as something positive born out of the tragedy of her short life.

I drink my tea slowly, hands around the mug as though I'm cold. I think of my student self as I was when I met Leo, the great author. The aspirations I held back then, my own burning desire to write.

Leo fell for Tara's Sylvia Plath-esque magnetism – her suicide gene attractive in the same way some men like the jutting bones on an anorexic girl. He fell for me because I was ordinary, low maintenance. And because, content to admire his genius, I was no competition for the limelight. My notebook – and my literary pretentions – lay abandoned in a drawer.

That it was genius, there was no doubt. *The Knife Edge* was a harrowing but absorbing and multi-layered book. I was fascinated by his ability to get inside Tara's head, Tara who was apparently so complicated.

I had always assumed he found getting into my mind comparatively easy.

The envelope lies there, inert yet hypnotic.

On the front is written Leo's name – but not in Leo's handwriting. It is thin, spidery writing, scratchy and harsh. Tara's. I pull out the tattered, yellowing manuscript, knowing before I read the words exactly what they will say.

I stare at it for a long, long time, then slide the bundle of paper back inside.

The phone rings.

"Hello, gorgeous," says Leo, his voice low and resonant with the first speech of the morning.

"Hey."

"Everything OK? You sound tired." His words are soft, full of concern.

"There was a bit of a disaster in the night."

"Why? What's up, sweetheart?"

My heartbeat is staccato. "Jason and Natalie's flat flooded – the water came through the ceiling in your study."

"You went in there?" His tone has changed in an instant.

"Darling, we had to. There was water – "

"I told you never to go in there."

"It was an emergency."

"Never. I thought you understood that."

"I did, but – "

"You disobeyed me."

"For fuck's sake Leo – what? Are you worried I've spoilt your creative aura? Because believe me, there wasn't one."

Silence.

He can tell.

"What did you find?"

No, don't be silly. He can't. He can't tell. Of course he can't!

"There wasn't anything *to* find. The whole room was empty – if your clothes weren't still in the wardrobe, I might have thought you'd moved out."

I hear – or maybe feel – him let out a breath. He tries a laugh. "Yeah, I guess it does look a little stark. I just work better that way. You know – the sterility somehow makes me feel more creative."

I wonder if he truly believes this, or if the lie is just for my benefit.

"Jason rescued your laptop and the printer, so you won't have lost anything."

"Thanks darling." He pauses. "Sorry for going off at you – it's just so private."

"Forget it."

"I love you."

"Me too." The response is automatic but for the first time I doubt its truth.

I put the phone down.

From the study comes a slap and a thump. The ceiling has finally collapsed. I take the envelope, push open the study door, step over the towels and pieces of sodden plaster board.

I take a last glance at the front cover of the manuscript:

The Knife Edge by Tara Ballachey

I push the pages back into the envelope, and drop it back into the middle drawer. If it becomes papier-mâché, so much the better.

I shut the door, turn the key.

Back in the kitchen, I sit at the table and pull a pad and pen towards me. I start to write. The words spill onto the page faster and faster.

RASPBERRY RIPPLE

She sees him every Friday from the narrow window of her pokey office. Her desk is angled so that as she reaches for the next item in her in-tray, her eye is often caught by movement outside; the flash of a bird's wings, the lift and sway of the leaves on the trees, a shaft of sunshine spilling out from behind a cloud. She welcomes these brief something-nothing distractions, reminders of life beyond the apparent stasis of work.

She cannot be sure when she first began to be aware of him – the individual person of him, as opposed to merely his presence once a week in the standard blue polo shirt of the grounds staff. She has waitressed in the past, and is all too aware that once dressed in corporate attire – the black skirt/white blouse of the waitress, the unflattering scrubs of the nurse, the luminous tabard of the steward – the person inside becomes miraculously invisible. She is annoyed with herself for her blindness which seems at best careless, at worst, rude.

*

He wonders what it must be like to work inside, to spend the majority of your day arse glued to a chair. He has always worked outside, buffeted by the wind, fried by the sun, or stung by rain, as nature's mood dictates. Whatever goes on within the buildings on the business park is a mystery to him. If he bothers to think of it at all, it is with a mixture of awe and contempt. Those who fly their desks every day have the fat comfort of their education behind them, the badge that says to others of their type that they belong. They sit in their offices, or in meetings, and fill their days with emails, phone calls, and words, words, words. He much prefers the solidity of his own work, fingers immersed in the rich, friable soil, or wielding hedge-cutters, leaf-blowers, strimmers, and sprayers.

Wherever he's working of a morning, he likes to pause to watch the office staff arriving. By the time they pull into the car park in their sleek vehicles, he and the other maintenance staff have usually been at work for an hour or so. The women tip tap in on uncomfortable looking heels. The men stride by wearing crisp suits, jangling their car keys, and talking in strident voices on their mobile phones. They all walk and talk double quick time, fighting their way through the day. It makes him smile. They expend so much energy, and yet here they are every morning, back where they started.

On Fridays, when he sees her, she's always alone. She looks, not miserable exactly, but locked in on herself. She is tall, but walks as if she wishes otherwise, sliding as inconspicuously as possible into the side entrance of her building, and appearing briefly, moments later, as a shadow in the narrow window, shrugging off her coat, and leaning across the desk to switch on her computer.

After that, she is mainly out of sight. Occasionally if he's working on the flower bed across the path, he'll catch a glimpse of her pale face, staring blankly out of the window. Once he thought she was looking right at him, and he risked a smile, but she merely looked away.

*

The abstract thought of him – his stature, his presence – begins to seep into her mind, creeping across the pages of her work, the screen of her computer. On Fridays, she finds her hands stilled on the keyboard, the cursor flashing expectantly.

But when he smiles in at her through the window one afternoon, she is mortified, as though he has somehow caught her out. The expression in his eyes is bright and amused. She keeps her own expression neutral and makes her glance slide back to the computer screen until he passes by. His proximity, his reality, has intruded on her daydreams of him, making her feel foolish.

As if he would be interested in her! He who is so, so practical, while she just sits there, incubating headaches and amassing paper cuts. How dull she must seem to him! How lifeless, how ordered, when he seems all energy and strength. She tries not to watch him as he passes by. But her eyes betray her.

*

He tells himself she is not his type. His past girlfriends have been lively, fun loving, preened and made up; warm in personality and flesh. This woman is aloof and self-contained, almost a shadow.

Yet, every Friday morning, he finds himself going the long way around the building, taking the path which passes directly under her window. Sometimes he risks glancing in, but all he sees is his own reflection in the scrupulously clean window pane.

He imagines her going home in the evening to a show-home-clean and perfect house. Preparing herself a nutritious, well-balanced meal in her sparkling TV-ad kitchen. Going to…what did women like her do in the evenings? Pilates? The theatre?

He pictures taking her home to his rented two-up, two-down, with the worn carpet and the faint smell of dog (long after the dog's demise). Eating take-out on their laps on the soggy sofa in front of the telly. Taking her to bed with the rumpled sheets and the joysticks for the old games console hanging over the footboard. The thought is so ridiculous, he feels the smile stretching across his face. Impossible.

*

She hasn't had a boyfriend since Ed walked out on her. It had not been love on either side, but the absence of him was at first so debilitating she thought she might be genuinely ill. The weight dropped off her. Her wrist bones stuck out like marbles. Her hair lay lank around her pallid face.

But all that emotion has run its course, wound down like a clockwork toy. Her mind and body have become still. The only images which come, unbidden, into her head are those of a blue polo shirt clad figure, tending his borders.

In her pokey kitchen, she stands on one leg, the other bent, foot resting against her opposite knee, eating a microwave meal for one. She tries to imagine him here in the flat with her, the bulk of him sandwiched in between the galley style units. Taking him through to the lounge where a fussy throw hides the uncomfortable sofa she never uses. Blushing at the pretention of the two upright fireside chairs where there is no fire. Watching him glance at the looming wall of books, the spilling pile of magazines she keeps meaning to catch up with, the bills and bank statements she'll one day get round to filing. She wants to put a protective arm around the room, and hug it to her. Cannot bear the thought of an intruder's eye making it ugly.

*

He finds himself weeding the border outside her window just before 9 o'clock one Friday morning. He tells himself this time he'll say hello. Look up, give her a big smile, and say, 'hello'. What's so difficult? How can it not have happened before?

Each time he hears voices or footsteps, his head snaps round to check, but it's never her. The hands on his watch crawl round to nine. He finishes the border, which is, in any case, the most over-tended of any on the business park, but stays crouched, pulling at the odd brown leaf or any other imperfection he can find. Waiting.

At ten past he realises she will not come. She's never late. She must have the day off. Perhaps she's had the whole week. The thought of her absence lies over him like a sodden blanket. He pushes himself unwillingly upright, takes his fork and sack of weeds, and trudges away.

*

It is gone 11 o'clock when she slips through the side door. Her jaw is aching, the injection wearing off now so that the pain is beginning to surface like a low level buzz in her brain. She is relieved he's not there to witness her lopsided smile, the likelihood of drool. She tells herself she needs to look after herself more, not let things like the dentist slide until there's an emergency. The lack of sleep, and the hangover of pain makes her fuzzy. She wishes he would come and wrap his arms around her, hold her up. Wishes, and yet is relieved when there is no sign of him.

She does all the essential work, and asks to leave early, telling herself it's coincidence that she is walking past the maintenance van with the blue logo just around his knocking off time. Her heart drums in her chest. But he is not there.

*

The soles of his boots have left a tell-tale trail of soil down the perfectly tiled aisle. He kicks a clod of mud guiltily against the edge of the chiller cabinet, chucks a couple of pizzas in his basket and scoots into the next aisle.

She is standing in front of the ice-cream section, scanning the selection over and over.

"Raspberry ripple," he says, over her shoulder.

She jumps, turns, flushes and grins all in the space of a second. "You think?"

She is holding one hand almost to her lips. He fights the desire to kiss her.

"Definitely. What other flavour is there?"

He is talking to her. They are talking. Just like that. So easy.

She says, "I don't usually buy ice-cream, but after the dentist, I thought it might be soothing."

He half thinks of offering to take her for a drink somewhere, but standing there in his scruffy work gear, he is aware of the slightly stale smell of manual labour clinging to his skin, the ground in dirt around his nails and in the lines of his calloused hands.

Instead he does a sympathetic wince. "Raspberry ripple. Have you right in no time." He winks and walks off before she has time to smell him.

*

She sits in one fireside chair, her feet propped up on the other, spooning raspberry ripple ice-cream slowly from the tub. The pain has dulled. She can't be sure if it's the ice-cream or something else.

If she kept a journal – which she hasn't done for years – she knows that life up to this moment would be punctuated by a big fat full-stop. And now she wants to turn the page.

*

The hedge trimmers slice through the foliage, scattering the new growth like fallen infantrymen. He cannot believe how much everything has grown in the space of a week. Spring is giving way to summer, and nature is bursting with energy. A wild rose climbing up through the branches falls victim to the blade and tumbles to the ground. He stares at the pink petals, silences the hedge trimmers, and bends to retrieve the fallen flower.

He feels the burden of stasis weighing him down. The perpetuity of his life and hers existing separately, nothing more than a smile or a hello once a week, forever.

He straightens, turns, and his feet propel him towards her window, stepping under trees, across bark-chip paths, between borders.

He taps on the glass. Sees her flinch and look up; her

confused smile. She stands, the office chair rolling back on its wheels, and leans across the desk to open the narrow window. But the frame has been painted shut over the years and it won't budge.

She gives him a helpless smile, gestures for him to hold on.

*

Embarrassment floods through her as she stands awkwardly before him. She's panting a little, making it obvious she's run. She holds one hand at the base of her throat to cover the creeping flush.

His eyes are huge and bright, and it occurs to her that he too is breathing a little heavily. Something inside her untwists.

He holds out the rose, its subtle pink petals uplifted towards her. When she takes it from him, their fingers brush.

She feels the page turn, and waits for the start of the next sentence.

GOING SOLO

There were no seats. In Judy's day, when you were waiting for a train, they would have at least provided seats. The platform was thick with people. Even pressed back against the wall, her bags gathered at her feet, Judy felt exposed and jostled. In the distance, she could make out a single metal bench, but it was already occupied, and in any case, she hardly felt like carting her things all the way up there, only to have to cart them all the way back when the train came.

She had too many bags. She'd expected a porter and maybe a trolley, but there'd been no-one to ask. The taxi driver had been a dear – helping her carry everything onto the concourse. But he couldn't leave his cab standing there with the engine running, so after she'd paid him and waved him off, she was on her own.

There was a steady stream of people thumping down the steps and onto the platform. So many people. She couldn't quite believe it. It had been a long time since she'd travelled by train. She'd been spoilt during her married life – Bill had driven her everywhere. She wasn't used to this hustle and bustle. Everyone nowadays seemed to be tapping away at their phones, or plugged into their headphones, wires trailing into pockets or bags. And no-one spoke. They merely glanced at the information screen, before pushing through to find a gap where they could stand.

Judy tried to pull her bags closer around her feet, conscious of being in the way. Too many bags. And yet, not enough. There were so many precious things she'd not been able to carry. Anna had arranged for a company to come and collect the furniture – the bits that would fit in the annex. She'd been quite specific about what Judy would be able to bring. Judy had already said farewell to that lovely old table with the barley twist legs. And the piano had to go of course. Anna said it was good to have a clear out. She'd called it de-cluttering. The remaining furniture had been spread out around the house in the newly vacant spaces. Anna had said it was important to "stage" the rooms to entice would-be purchasers. When Judy had left her old home that morning, the house already looked like it belonged to someone else.

Thirty-five years Judy had lived in the three bed semi. Thirty-four of those years with Bill. The loss of him had settled to something akin to a long-term tooth ache. Some of the time she was able to ignore it and get on with things normally. Other times, often in the evenings after tea, she would be overwhelmed by longing for him. Bill, so solid and unruffled. He wouldn't have stood for this – Anna making all the decisions, Anna telling her what was best.

The Tannoy blared somewhere above her head. There was a delay of some sort. Judy couldn't be sure if it related to her train or not, but she saw expressions of annoyance on the faces around her and assumed it was. She'd have to stand a while longer then. Her feet hurt. She'd worn her best shoes, wanting to look decent for the journey, but they weren't the most comfortable for walking. She could feel a place on her heel that was hot and sore.

Most of the people around her looked grey and fed up, anxious to be on their way. A little to her right though,

Judy saw a young couple, students probably, talking earnestly, their bodies gravitating towards one another like magnets. The boy seemed unable to take his eyes off the girl. The girl kept glancing down the platform unhappily.

Despite Judy's aching feet, she found she welcomed the delay. She was happy to stand a while longer. Perhaps if she stood here long enough, she'd fossilize and not ever have to move again. She often felt like that. Wanting to be still, to not be tossed around by someone else's will.

It dawned on her that she did not want to go to Anna's. Surprisingly, the thought had not previously crystallised in her mind. She had fooled herself that it was the herculean task of the move itself which was filling her heart with gloom. But now she made herself focus on what lay in store for her. Travelling down to Anna's clinically clean executive home, the hermetically sealed, double glazed rooms, the cream carpets on which you were not allowed to set foot until you'd removed your shoes. And then there was the fact of being a permanent guest in someone else's home. Oh, of course, Anna had said it wouldn't be like that – she should treat the place as her own – but Judy knew that would be impossible. She would creep about, unable to settle to any task, constantly hoping she didn't mess up something.

It hadn't always been like this. Judy would once have said her relationship with her daughter was excellent, more like two friends on an equal footing, not parent and child. But over the years, Anna seemed to have hardened, had become fonder of telling Judy what she should be doing, how she ought to be managing. Now that Bill was gone, it seemed impossible to avoid her dominance.

Judy felt a pang. She was doing Anna an injustice. After all, it was extremely kind of her to offer a place in her own home. To take from her the responsibility of direct debits, and meter readings, and maintenance, and all the other things she was so poor at dealing with simply because they had always been Bill's domain. Anna said Judy should now be free to enjoy her retirement. But Judy feared this would morph into a retirement not just from work, but from life itself. Would she end up just sitting in the square, featureless annex of the executive home, gazing blankly out of the window and wondering what to do with herself?

And then there was Anna's husband, Ray. If she was honest, Judy had never quite taken to Ray. There was something distasteful about his brash over-confidence. When he'd come with Anna to visit in the past, he'd seemed too large for the house. He was always toppling ornaments, or scuffing the edges of rugs, and he managed to make these things seem like the fault of the house, not his own clumsiness. Judy assumed that the size of the executive home was necessary to prevent him from perpetually ricocheting off door frames and into items of furniture.

Bill had been a tall man, and muscular too in his day, but he'd also had a lithe agility which Judy had never tired of admiring. He never had any trouble navigating around their home without causing havoc. His presence had always been a comforting constant. For weeks after he'd died, Judy had thought she'd heard his tread on the stair, or the faint sound of his whistling coming from some other room. Would his ghost travel with her to Anna's sterile home? She somehow doubted it.

A man stepped back into her, treading on one of her bags and leaving a dirty footprint on the fabric. He muttered an automatic apology and moved on before Judy could respond. The platform was filled with a heavy swell of bodies, dangerously hoisted rucksacks and unwieldy shopping bags. The young couple were now holding hands in a gesture that seemed more of desperation than love.

The Tannoy erupted into life again, the blurred announcement confirming the delayed train was finally on its approach. The tide of bodies pressed and heaved around Judy and she started to gather her belongings. Only the young couple remained static.

The dirty yellow lights of the train glowed in the gloom, and the carriages clanked and screeched their way into the station, rumbling to a halt with a hiss and a thump.

Without waiting for passengers to disembark, the press of bodies on the platform pushed forwards towards the doors. Judy felt herself stagger as she was carried by the tide. The handle of one of her bags slipped from her grasp and she let out a little cry of panic. She fought the onslaught of bodies, standing her ground in her best shoes, hunching herself against the battering of shoulders and elbows and shopping bags.

Her fingers closed round the bag handle, and she pulled it close to her, breathing heavily. The lava flow of people oozed around the obstacle of Judy and her luggage and onto the train, filling every available gap, pushing up against the windows, packing everyone in.

Judy saw the girl from the couple standing in the doorway of the carriage, still holding her boyfriend's hand. He was refusing to let go. They were staring at each other, wide-eyed and fearful.

The lights around the doors began to flicker, and an urgent beeping warned they were about to close. The girl jumped back onto the platform, her cheeks flushed, her eyes bright. The boy pulled her into his arms.

The doors rumbled shut. Judy's heart turned over.

The train began to inch forwards. Only Judy and the young couple were left on the platform. She felt the pent up panic and dread inside slowly leak away. She stood in her island of luggage, and felt Bill smile down at her.

She was still holding her seat reservation in her hand, crumpled and sweaty. Coach E, seat 49. She hoped someone deserving had taken her place.

She picked up her bags, and turned to the escalator. She needed to find a phone, warn Anna she wouldn't be coming. Not on this train, or any other. And then she would hail another taxi and go back to what was left of her home.

SKIN DEEP

I am all but invisible. If the women who come here notice anything about me it will be my neat, swept up hair, my soft clean hands, my accent. I notice everything about them. They arrive with ashen faces, weary from their stressful jobs or demanding families, their nails broken and bitten, their muscles knotted. I caress and sooth, exfoliate and moisturise, preen and beautify, and wonder what happens when they go home. How long does the glow of relaxation, or the joy of their new found beauty, take to wear off?

One of the clients - we will call her Rosalind - is stick thin, beyond slender. Her eyes are huge, and so beautifully made up that I feel guilty when she has a facial and I must sweep it all away with those cotton wool pads.

I say, "It is better, after this treatment, to leave the moisturiser on - no make-up. Yes?"

She nods, and gives a small smile, but I know that before she leaves the Spa, the perfect make-up will have been re-applied. The beauty mask in place before she returns home.

The other girls joke about our lengthy training courses -

say that by this time we ought to be doctors or lawyers! I don't tell them that once upon a time I imagined such a future. They would laugh. People like me do not become doctors or lawyers. I am lucky to have avoided waitressing, cleaning, or worse. I take my hard-won certificates, and like the other girls, blend into the background.

It is peaceful in my small square treatment room, music tinkling softly in the background. The women blow in like leaves, each momentarily swirling and blustering, before coming to rest. They are all different and yet all the same. Some are loud and demanding; everything is too hot, too cold, brought them out in a rash last time. The others are mousy quiet; blush at being touched, almost wish the ordeal over, even though it is supposed to be a treat.

The regulars are the ones with money - sometimes their own, often they've married it. I wonder if it makes them happy. I think not. It must be disappointing to imagine wealth will make everything right, and to discover it does not.

Rosalind is one of these ladies, I think. Sometimes she has a massage. A few times she has booked one, but changes her mind on the day.

I say, "You do not want? But you will be charged anyway?"

Her large eyes glisten and she shakes her head.

One day while I am massaging her shoulders, a drop of oil begins to roll from her left shoulder blade down her back. I move the towel slightly to catch the drip with my fingertips, and that is when I notice the ring of fresh puckered skin. A small circular burn. My heart stops, though my fingers - well-trained - continue stroking. As they slide over the jutting wings of her shoulder blades, over the nodules of her vertebrae, my eye is constantly drawn to that angry red mark.

I say nothing. But I feel a thousand screaming voices building inside me. I want her shoulder blade wings to flap wildly and fly her away from danger.

When I have finished, I pull up the towel, and say I will leave her to dress in her own time.

I slip outside, shutting the door softly.

In the staff room, I wash my hands and stare at myself in the mirror. I think of all the people who will have pretended not to notice. I think of the miles I have travelled to escape such things, only to discover they are everywhere. Even the beautiful woman in my treatment room has been made to feel she is not enough.

I apply a little more cover-up over the faintly visible scar on my neck, wipe my hands on a paper towel, and hurry back to the treatment room.

Rosalind has gone.

Weeks go by. I begin to think Rosalind will not come again. I half think to say something. I ask my boss what you say is a hypothetical question. What should I do if? But my boss says I should not worry about the customers, just look after myself. These are difficult times, she says, for women like me, who've come to work in the UK, who've left a whole other life behind. The future is uncertain.

My boss is a good woman. She will do her best for me and for the other girls, I know this, but the dreams come again. I wake suffocating in the bed clothes. For a moment I think I am back there. Back with him. The air is poisonous; I am made ugly in his eyes.

When I can breathe again, I promise myself: never again.

One morning, I collect my client list and Rosalind's name jumps off the page. Relief surges through me. My hands shake while I prepare the room.

She has booked a facial. When she comes in, she is wearing a smile like a magician's flourish, but I am not taken in. She lies on the couch, settles her head back, and I begin to take off the make-up. The foundation is thick, and I see why. The ghost of a blue shadow appears under my stroking cotton pad. I pause. She shuts her eyes. I go on.

The bruise is huge. It covers her left cheekbone all the way up to her eye socket, which is as swollen as an overripe fruit. I take extra care to be as gentle as possible, but still I see her flinch. When all the make-up is gone, the livid blue looks evil against her naturally pale skin.

I stop, my hands resting lightly on her shoulders.

She tries to look up at me, but it is impossible from the angle of the headrest. Instead she reaches up, puts her right hand over my left one.

I lean forward and place a kiss on the huge livid bruise.

She shuts her eyes, and a tear slides out from beneath her dark lashes.

At first she says it is impossible. He will find her, make her go back. I tell her this is not so, not if you want enough to leave. I tell her about my own flight. She listens, chewing her lip, her huge eyes cast downwards as though to meet my gaze will force her to accept my words as the truth. She is terrified. I take her hand in mine; quiet the tremor, tell her it will be OK.

She builds a pile of objections between us; she has no money of her own, no job, cannot contribute, she will make trouble for her family. I sweep the objections away with a wave of my hand. I'm happy to share my flat and my income - small though they are. Her family would not want her to stay just to keep some imagined peace. I will keep her safe until he gives up looking for her.

She looks up at last, and though she is silent, her eyes say yes.

When it comes to it, she is brave and courageous. She leaves her car (his car) parked at the railway station, and buys a ticket on his credit card to some random destination several hours away. She goes to the public toilets and gets changed in one of the cubicles. If there is CCTV in operation, it will record someone completely different walking out of the station and towards town. If her husband tries to track her phone, it's in a sanitary bin.

A few minutes later, she joins the queue at a bus stop. I am already in the queue; I have my headphones in, as though I'm listening to music, deep in thought. We do not acknowledge one another. When the bus comes, we climb aboard. She sits in the seat behind mine. My skin prickles, she is so close.

When I get up at my stop, she waits a heartbeat then comes to stand behind me. The bus pulls in, the doors swish open and I step out. I hear her thank the driver, her voice soft and sweet as always. I don't turn, but keep walking. I make a show of messing with my phone, picking a new track from my song list. But the only thing I listen to is the sound of her footsteps a short distance behind me.

At the entrance to my block, I pause to make sure she has time to see me go in, then head on up the stairs. I put my key in the lock, push open the door and wait. It's probably less than 30 seconds before she follows me inside, but it feels like a lifetime.

Only when I turn and shut the door do we finally allow ourselves to look at each other. She is shaking, but her eyes are filled with fire. When I pull her into my arms, she clings on as if she were drowning.

I am all but invisible to the clients, but I don't care. I don't envy them, I feel compassion. For them, going home means going back to whatever drove them to the Spa in the first place. When I go home to the tiny flat, I am going to my own personal heaven; I am going home to Rosalind.

We have no money, but we have each other. Rosalind does not mourn her grand house, her fast car or her expensive clothes, because the price for such things is too high.

When it is just the two of us, we do not worry about covering up our scars. They chart our journey and they are a part of who we are. They say beauty is only skin deep but anyone in love knows otherwise.

LUCK OF THE DRAW

Ruth threw down her pen.

"It's no use. I can't do this. It's impossible to come up with a seating plan which won't end up with at least two of our guests killing each other!"

Lizzy made a face. "If I thought anyone was likely to create a scene at my wedding, I wouldn't invite them in the first place!"

"That's what I said at the outset." Ruth chewed a nail and gazed blankly at the seating plan. "I was adamant. No one we didn't really want to be there – no one we just felt obliged to invite. But then Phil invited the three guys from his office he really gets on with, and there's only one other lad there, so he had to invite him even though no one really likes him. And of course, he said 'yes' which Phil wasn't expecting. And then there's all my lot."

Liz looked at her sideways. "You've never invited Tory?"

"I had to, didn't I?"

"Ruthee! What were you thinking?"

"Oh, what does it matter? It was all about a hundred years ago."

"But Tory!" said Lizzy, "At your wedding?"

Ruth pushed a hand up through her hair. It felt limp and lifeless, just as she did. When she'd started planning the wedding, she'd expected it to be fun, but now the whole thing felt like a monstrously heavy burden.

"It'll be fine. It's not like there's anything between us anymore," she said. "Besides, it's done now. I can't un-invite him."

"And he's definitely coming?"

"Yes. He sent a card." Ruth reached across for the file box where she kept all the wedding arrangement paraphernalia. Her hand found the envelope too easily. She tried not to look at the handwriting of her address, but remembered how startled she'd been when it had appeared in the post. "Here."

"Flattered to be asked; delighted to attend, T," Liz read. "Huh! Only Tory could find the need for a semi-colon in an RSVP." She held the card for a moment longer, then pushed it back into the envelope. "Perhaps he'll change his mind. You know, something might come up - like it always seemed to - and he won't come."

Ruth made a face

"Oh God," said Liz, "If he turns up, it'll ruin everything."

Ruth sat back on her heels and looked Lizzy straight in the eye. "No it won't. I love Phil, and I'm going to marry him. A million Torys couldn't change that."

Liz looked for a moment as if she was going to say something else, then held up her hands. "Alright, alright. If you're sure." She frowned. "Anyway, on the phone you said there was another problem. What was that?"

"Favours! We'd ordered these really cute handmade wooden love spoons - we were expecting them any day, and then this morning I got an email saying the place which makes them has gone out of business. So what do I do now?"

Liz shrugged. "Just buy some sugared almonds and stick them in those little organza bags."

"Ugh! That's so twee! It's not 1980! I wanted some kind of little trinket to give everyone."

Lizzy wrinkled her nose. "Whatever you give out, you're just obliging everyone to either keep theirs forever, or chuck it into landfill. Not very ethical."

Ruth rolled her eyes. "OK, so what do you suggest?"

"How about lottery tickets?"

"Huh?"

"Buy every guest a lottery ticket. The wedding's on a Saturday – so do it for that evening's draw. Of course, no one will win, but it'll give your guests a bit of excitement, plus the tickets can go in the recycling at the end of the evening!"

Ruth grinned. "Genius! Lottery tickets it is."

"You'll get one for us too, won't you?" Phil lay on the bed, propped up on one elbow watching Ruth laying out the table plan on the duvet in front of her.

"Hmm?"

"Lottery ticket."

"Oh, yeah. Of course. Not that I need one." She shot him a sideways glance. "I'm as happy as if I'd already won the lottery."

Phil grinned, stretched out his hand and pulled her towards him, planting a kiss firmly on her lips.

Ruth giggled. "Watch it – you'll crush the table plan!"

Phil let her go and turned the plan towards him.

"What do you think?" asked Ruth.

"Seems fine. Doesn't matter to us if the rest of the guests squabble – we'll be on top table."

"That's not really the point."

Phil squinted closer at the plan. "Is 'Tory' a boy or a girl?"

The sound of his name on Phil's lips was like two worlds colliding. Ruth felt her heart skitter. "Boy. Victor really, but no-one ever calls him that."

"One of your Uni mates I take it, given you've put him

on the same table as Maddie and that crowd."

Ruth made a noise of assent.

"And is he?"

"Is he what?"

"A tory? True blue? Tim-nice-but-dim?"

A picture of Tory as he had been in their university days came unbidden into her mind. His dark, unkempt, curly hair. His blue, blue eyes. The eclectic assortment of clothes he wore which on anyone else would have looked scruffy, but on his slender frame, became effortlessly stylish. If he'd been an item of furniture, he'd have been shabby chic.

"Hardly. His dad probably was. Tory was more of an eco-freak back then. But who knows?" Ruth pulled the table plan back towards her. Maybe Tory would have evolved into a typical middle class, middle manager, with a paunch and an executive home on a housing estate. He'd arrive at the hotel in a BMW and bore people with boardroom tittle tattle. A bit of her hoped for this. It would make everything so much easier.

Phil took the paper out of her hand, and dropped it over the side of the bed.

"Enough wedding guff," he said, "I want to spend some quality time with the future Mrs Griffiths."

The solidity of his body against hers was absolute. She put her arms around him and pulled him to her. His kiss blotted out everything. Even Tory.

Going down the aisle, she felt blind. In the sea of faces on either side of her, she could pick out no-one. Her dad's arm through hers felt steady and solid, though she knew he was probably equally nervous, and she clung to him. If Tory was there, in the congregation somewhere, she couldn't see him.

As they reached the front, Freddie, Phil's best man, gave her a wink and a thumbs-up. She grinned and immediately knew everything was going to be ok.

When they got to the part about the lawful impediment, there was the briefest of pauses, filled with a single cough from somewhere in the congregation. The cough made her jump, but there was nothing else, and the ceremony continued to its conclusion.

It was during the photographs that she saw him. She'd lent down to rest the bouquet on a low wall while she righted her veil which had caught briefly in a gust of wind. He had his back to her, talking to Maddie and another of her old uni mates. He was wearing a mildly creased linen suit, and it was the suit and something about the angle of his shoulders which convinced her that it was Tory.

"Everything ok?" asked Lizzy, picking up the bouquet and helping to drape the veil correctly over her shoulders.

"Absolutely," said Ruth.

Lizzy's eye narrowed and she glanced over her shoulder. "Uh-o."

"Come on," said Ruth briskly, "Bride and Bridesmaids – all the girls."

Of course, she knew she would have to speak to him at some point. She couldn't very well invite him and then ignore him for the whole of the day. In her daydreams about this moment, she was always in the middle of a witty conversation with one of Phil's good looking work colleagues; Tory would be hovering in the background, waiting to speak to her, and she'd turn and bestow upon him a beatific smile, and say something like, "Oh, Tory, sorry, I didn't see you there." And he, humbled by her beauty, would be tongue-tied. And, oh yes, fatter. Much fatter. And with no hair.

When it actually happened, she'd just come out of the ladies toilet, and was trying to stop her underskirt digging into her hipbone.

"Wardrobe malfunction?"

He was leaning against a pillar with a glass of champagne in each hand. The sound of his voice made something tumble down inside her. She felt clammy inside her starchy dress.

"No, it's fine," she said, though it was not. She forced an over-bright smile.

He held out one of the glasses, which she took, unwillingly. The action seemed to make her beholden to him somehow. Yet it would have been churlish not to accept a drink.

"To the stunning bride," he said, managing to hold her gaze as he clinked glasses and drank deeply. "Phil's a lucky man."

She wanted to slap him. For the cliché, and for the ease with which he said it.

"Isn't he?" she said.

Tory gave a wry smile, and twirled the stem of his now empty champagne flute in his fingertips. Unfortunately he had not got fat, though he seemed to her more solid, no longer a slender boy but a muscular man. He still had all his hair, and of course those dangerous blue eyes.

"Are you happy, Ruth?"

"Yes." She looked at him squarely. "Are you?"

He laughed. "My happiness is almost within touching distance - but sadly, no."

He pushed himself away from the pillar, planted a sudden kiss on her cheek, and strolled back towards the function room.

Lizzy's eyes narrowed when Ruth joined her once more. "So you've seen him then?"

"Who?" asked Ruth.

"Don't give me that. I can tell by your expression. You're all lit up."

"I'm all lit up because it's my wedding day."

Lizzy made a face, so Ruth made one back at her and, giving a theatrical twirl, went off to mingle. Lizzy was right of course. She felt lit up. As if the spotlight of his gaze was on her as she sashayed around the room enjoying the weight of the dress, the way the material clung and spun as she walked. Phil caught her eye across the room and she went to stand by him, their arms around each other. But all the time it felt like a display, a piece of self-conscious acting. She wanted Tory to be watching, seeing how happy she was, cursing himself for letting her go.

When it came to the first dance, Phil, awkward and unwilling, pulled her onto the dance floor, and shuffled, foot to foot, out of rhythm in front of her, his hands holding hers, dragging at her, as if she were a buoy and he was drowning. Ruth tried not to imagine how it would have been with Tory. Dancing with Tory all those years ago had just worked. It was as though their bodies had been joined by a length of invisible rope which kept them together as they moved about the dance floor. They had instinctively picked up on each other's cues for turns and spins, for dancing alone and then coming together again.

Ruth tried to pull Phil into her arms and inject a bit of sparkle into their dance. Phil was so confident in other ways, and fit and sporty, so she couldn't understand why he was so leaden on the dancefloor. Their mates had always teased him about it, so he avoided dancing whenever possible, and she knew this was a bit of an ordeal for him. Even so, she couldn't help wishing they didn't look so clunky together.

Mercifully, the song began to draw to a close, and the DJ urged others to join the happy couple for something a little more upbeat. On the prompt side of social acceptability, Phil gave Ruth a clumsy hug, and then slid away to the edge of the dancefloor, turning the whole thing into a joke, briefly dancing with Freddie. Ruth was about to follow him off the floor when five year old Ellie, Phil's niece, their flower girl, launched herself into Ruth's arms, and begged her to dance.

After Phil's obvious awkwardness, Ellie's enthusiasm was infectious, and soon Ruth was spinning the little girl around, and copying a range of moves far too undignified for someone in a formal dress. She was giggling and breathless by the time the music changed to something more slow and melodic.

Ellie said with comical directness, "I need a wee." And hitching up her dress, she ran straight off across the dancefloor in the direction of the toilets.

"Cute."

Tory stood easily beside her, watching the little girl depart.

The world went very slightly out of kilter, then righted itself.

He said, "Would it be terribly inappropriate for me to dance with the bride?"

"Terribly." She felt the inevitability of it all, the sliding towards the edge of the precipice.

He gave that old boyish grin, and reached for her hand, holding her by her little finger. The gesture was so painfully nostalgic, Ruth wanted to snatch her hand away, but to do so would have acknowledged it meant something.

They started to move, little more than swaying to the rhythm at first, but already it was as if his body was calling out to hers. She half wanted to stop, get off the dancefloor, and go and find Phil. But she couldn't. Tory lifted an arm very gently to settle round her waist. They moved together. And it all fitted, perfectly.

"Come on, mate, you can't monopolise the beautiful bride all evening." Freddie cut in and immediately pulled her into an elaborate spin.

The shock of it made her giggle like a school kid.

"That's better," said Freddie, "Can't have you looking all tragic on your wedding day."

"Tragic? Was I?"

"Looked like you needed rescuing." Freddie gave her another of his trademark heavy winks.

"Thanks," she said.

And it was true, she had indeed needed rescuing,

though not in the way Freddie had suggested.

"Have you seen that lot?" said Ruth, gesturing at the university crowd all gathered over Maddie's phone. "On the internet at our wedding! Bet they're on Facebook!"

"Nope. They're checking the lottery numbers," said Phil. He pulled his new wife into his arms and kissed the top of her head. "It's your own fault. You're the one who bought the tickets."

"It was Lizzy's idea."

"Do I hear my name being used in vain?" Lizzy appeared, grinning at them.

"Why aren't you over there with that horrible rabble, checking your numbers?" said Phil.

Lizzy did a little twirl, holding her gold envelope aloft. "No need - I've definitely got the winner right here. I can feel it in my water."

"You mean, in your gin," said Ruth.

"Anyway," said Phil, "Where's ours?"

Ruth laughed.

"No, seriously!" Phil look pointedly at Ruth, as though she was going to produce a ticket from the stiff bodice of her dress.

"We haven't got one."

"What? Why on earth not?" said Phil.

"You did have one," said Lizzy. "I know, I was there when you bought them."

"Yup, but then Auntie Mags who'd originally said she couldn't come, because there was no-one to look after Mr Tiddles while she was away, suddenly changed her mind."

"How come?" said Phil. "What happened to Mr Tiddles?"

Ruth made a face. "Squished."

"Ouch!" said Lizzy.

"Yes, poor Tiddles."

"Poor us too," said Phil. "We might have won a fortune."

"I don't care about a fortune," said Ruth. "I've got you."

"Well, that's lovely. But frankly, a few million quid would be nice too. This wedding didn't come cheap. And, you know I completely agree that it's old fashioned to expect the parents to cough up but I wasn't expecting us to be taking on something equivalent to the National Debt!"

Lizzy laughed.

"Phil! You old miser!" said Ruth, punching him lightly. "It's our wedding day! Besides, we've hardly been extravagant - you wouldn't have wanted it to be anything less than perfect, would you?"

"Ruthee, I wouldn't have cared if we'd had a Registry Office bash, and run away to Bognor," said Phil. "I just wanted to marry the most amazing woman I've ever met."

Ruth felt her eyes prick with tears. "That's the loveliest thing you've ever said!"

"I know. Smooth, wasn't it?" Phil winked at Lizzy. "She's a lucky gal, you know!'

Ruth put her arms around his neck, giggling. "Aren't I just?"

There was a sudden whoop of joy behind them which made them pull apart and turn to look.

"Twenty-five quid," shouted Freddie! "Get in!"

While she clapped and cheered along with everyone else, Ruth spotted Tory standing detached at the back of the group. He was staring at the three of them, his expression inscrutable.

She snapped her eyes away from him, and instinctively put her arm around Phil's waist.

The DJ drawled, "And I think we have a winner."

'Yes,' thought Ruth, 'but it's not Freddie.' She gave Phil a squeeze. 'I'm the real winner.'

"We've left all the cards and gifts on that back table," said the hotel's events manager, unlocking the function room door.

"Thanks - we completely forgot about them when we went up to our room last night." Ruth felt oddly detached from the world this morning. She wasn't hungover, just tired, but her limbs didn't feel entirely her own, and her head was fuzzy.

"I'll bring the car round to the front, and we'll load them all in," said Phil. "Unless you want to open them here?"

Ruth shook her head. "Let's wait until we get home."

"Right you are."

She watched Phil heading out of the door. My husband. It felt good. Strange, but good.

She turned back to the table, and sighed. It was awash with gifts, even though they'd said they had everything they needed. She didn't even feel equal to the task of opening them. Officially they had requested charitable donations but apparently Lizzy had created an alternative wedding list. There had been much giggling about this from their friends, and as Ruth peered into a large gift bag on the floor beside the table, she realised why. When Phil came back moments later, she moved the tissue paper aside, and showed him their first present: his and hers adult Space Hoppers.

"Go on - which one of 'em got us those?" he asked.

Ruth looked for the tag, but it merely said, Hope you'll always be able to keep the bounce in your relationship. There was no signature.

They checked the other tags. None of them were signed.

"Silly sods!" said Phil, grinning as he began to carry the gifts out to the car.

There was a huge pile of cards on the table. Ruth scooped them up, and as she did so, a small gold envelope slid out of the bundle. She picked it up - one of the party favour envelopes which had held the lottery tickets. The ticket was still inside. Probably one of the hotel staff had popped it on the pile by mistake. She turned the envelope over to see whose it was, but the little label she had made so painstakingly had been peeled off. Instead there was hand-written "R&P" on the front. She didn't recognise the writing.

"Phil, do you know what the lottery numbers were last night?" she asked as he came in for the next batch of parcels.

Phil put his hand to his head, shut his eyes and made a "wa-wa-wa" noise after the style of a 1970s Sci-Fi show. "Nope, can't get them."

"I meant on your phone, smart arse!" said Ruth.

"Why, has someone left us their winnings?" said Phil, eyeing the envelope.

"Not sure. My phone's in my bag. Have you got a signal?"

Phil frowned over the screen of his smart phone while he waited for the lottery page to upload.

"OK, first number is 12."

Ruth laughed. "Nope. Haven't got that!"

"Next one is 19."

"Ooh, yes. We've got that one."

Phil read out the next four numbers. They had them all.

"Bonus ball?"

"Three."

Ruth gave a little squeak.

"Don't tell me?"

"Five numbers and the bonus ball?"

"That's like..." Phil stabbed the screen. "Estimated £50,000."

"Fifty thousand pounds!"

Phil took the ticket and went through the numbers again. He looked up at Ruth and nodded.

"Right," said Ruth, very deliberately. "Let's not get too excited..."

"What?" said Phil, dropping his phone on the table and grabbing Ruth's hands. "No - let's get excited! Very excited!"

"But we still don't know whose ticket it was."

They were sitting on the floor in their lounge, drinking tea out of normal mugs. It was a relief after the local paper taking them back to the hotel to pose on the terrace with bottles of champagne. The photographer had even wanted them to change back into their wedding clobber, until Ruth pointed out that Phil's suit had to go back.

"We've been over this a million times," said Ruth. "No-one even knew anyone had won anything - well, other than Freddie."

"So it could be anyone other than Freddie?"

"Or Freddie - maybe he just lied about how much he'd won, you know, as cover."

Phil sniggered. "Na. Freddie's great, but he'd not give up that kind of money, even for me. It'll be your Auntie Mags, feeling bad because she stole our ticket."

"She'd have given it to the cats' home in memory of Mr Tiddles!" said Ruth.

"Maddie then. She doesn't need the money. She's loaded."

"She's not - well, only because she married Anton, whose father is something big in the city. If Maddie won, she'd have kept it, if only for a little independence."

"Hmm, maybe. But thinking about it, I did see her last night putting something on the gift table. I thought she was just adding a card to the pile, but she had a little smirk on her face like she was up to something."

"Really? I didn't notice."

"You were saying goodbye to all your work mates. When she turned away from the table, she caught me watching her. It was just for a moment. I thought she was going to come and say something, but she just gave me this funny smile and walked off."

Ruth felt a rush of warmth through her body. Suddenly she knew who'd left the ticket. Of course she knew. Who else would make such a grandiose gesture?

Tory.

"Tory?" Lizzy exclaimed. "Why would Tory have left you his ticket?"

"Because it's the ultimate gesture to prove how little he cares about money? To make us somehow beholden to him?" Ruth threw up her hands. "I don't know, I'll just have to go and find out."

"What?" The colour drained from Lizzy's face. "Why? You're just guessing it was him, and how will going to see him make anything better?"

Ruth stared out from the kitchen of Lizzy's tiny flat. It was a stiflingly hot day, and even with the window open as wide as it would go, the air was still. Ruth could feel her t-shirt sticking to her back.

"I've asked everyone else I can think of. No, I'm sure it's him. And it's like unfinished business if I don't speak to him about it."

"No!" said Lizzy. "Look, even if it was him, that's exactly what he'll want to happen. You'll be playing into his hands."

"I can't stop thinking about it."

"That'll be just because all the excitement of the wedding and the honeymoon is over."

Ruth made a face. "I couldn't stop thinking about it in Italy either."

"Oh, Ruth!" said Lizzy. "Look, this is hardly fair on Phil. You've only been married two minutes, and you're already filling your head with Tory."

"It's not like that. I want to get him out of my head. That's all."

Lizzy bit her lip. "As long as you're sure about that."

"Phil keeps asking why I don't want to spend any of the money." Ruth held her face towards the window. "He wants to do sensible stuff like pay off a big chunk of the mortgage, and I keep stalling. It's like once we've spent it,

Tory owns a bit of us, because really it's his money."

"But it isn't his money!" Lizzy protested. She paused. "He gave it to you. Plus, you know what he was always like about gambling and lottery wins and all that. He despised it all." She picked at a little piece of skin on the side of her fingernail. "It was one of the reasons I suggested the favours - I thought it would irritate him."

Ruth stared at her. "You wanted to get under his skin too."

Lizzy laughed bitterly. "Under it. Next to it. Whatever."

"*You* liked Tory?"

"Liked?" Lizzy stared ahead blankly. "Ruth... You're my best friend, and I love you dearly, but you can be really blind sometimes."

"But..." Ruth couldn't fit this new information into her brain. It was as though it was made of too many sticky-out bits to slot in with the other things she knew; thought she knew.

Lizzy gave a humourless laugh. "When I found out you'd invited him, I almost made an excuse not to come to the wedding. But I couldn't have done that to you. I just kept out of his way the whole day."

"You never said anything - all the time we were at uni." Ruth was running over so many past conversations, cringing. "Whenever we talked about him, you never said."

"And why do you think that was?"

Ruth looked at her best friend. Lizzy's fingers were grasping the edge of the worktop so tightly her fingers had gone white.

"It was always about you and Tory," said Lizzy. Her voice wobbled. "What he'd said to you this time. How he'd broken your heart yet again. How you knew he didn't love you the way you loved him. How you were sure there was someone else."

"You two weren't...?"

"For heaven's sake, Ruth! No, we bloody weren't. Don't you get it? I just hoped you'd eventually split up for good and then maybe someone else would stand a chance. Someone like me."

"But we did split up for good."

Lizzy gave a hollow laugh. "Be honest though. It was never very convincing, was it? I mean, you invited him to your wedding for heaven's sake!"

"What, and that doesn't prove we're over?"

Lizzy looked at her levelly. "For a while, I hoped that it did. And then I saw you after you'd spoken to him. It was like someone had run an electric current through you. You'll never be over. Not completely."

Ruth turned away, and walked the three short steps to the other side of the kitchen. It was as if someone had held up a mirror inside her brain. She saw herself clearly. And was ashamed. Bitterly ashamed.

The three steps back to Lizzy's side seemed a marathon. She loosed her friend's hands from the edge of the worktop and held them in her own.

"I am over him. Honestly. Yes, it was great to see him at the wedding - yes, he can still push those buttons, but it's not real. If it was going to be real, we'd have stayed together and I wouldn't have married Phil."

"Fine." Lizzy swallowed. "If that's the case, don't go and see him."

Ruth nodded. "OK. I won't."

She had meant to be as good as her word.

Her resolve had started off firm. She let Phil use some of the money to pay off their debts and a chunk of their mortgage. The rest they'd put in the bank. She wondered what they would ever agree to spend it on. Nothing seemed appropriate. The figures on their statement bothered her every time she logged into their internet banking. She tried to think of something Tory would approve of - but Tory and money were alien creatures. He would have given it all to a good cause. Maybe that's what he'd done. Maybe he'd considered her a good cause.

She would never have made the conscious decision to seek him out had she not, several weeks later, found herself driving back from a meeting held at head office. There'd been a smash on the motorway, and her satnav had taken her down a myriad of winding lanes as an alternative route. Stuck for a few minutes while a herd of cows slowly crossed the road in front of her, she was gazing at the route screen when she noticed the name of the adjacent village. It sounded familiar. She tried to tell herself she couldn't be sure of the address, but that was just self-deceit. She knew it.

By the time the cows had cleared, she'd made up her mind. She re-directed the satnav and nosed her way down the next winding lane, this time with her heart thudding into her chest.

When the satnav told her she'd reached her destination, she could hardly believe it.

"No wonder he could afford to give me his lottery ticket!" she said out loud.

Tory, it seemed, lived in a mansion.

She went to the front door first, but there was no such thing as a bell or a knocker, and when she tapped her knuckles against the monstrous old door, it was clear the sound would have been about as effective as a moth fluttering against the wood.

She almost lost courage, and was about to get back in the car when she thought she could faintly hear music. A guitar perhaps. She followed a slabbed path around the side of the house, nervously passing two enormous bay windows. A pair of dusky pink translucent curtains were pulled haphazardly across the first bay, and the second was dark, the room seemingly uninhabited but for a brindle coloured cat lying in the windowsill, which watched her pass and then yawned disinterestedly. Ruth caught her reflection in the glass, and felt depressingly suburban in her work suit.

At the back of the house there was a curious hotchpotch of garden furniture, along with some throws and cushions which had been laid out on the grass. These were wrinkled as though people had lolled on them until very recently. It took her a moment longer to notice that there was a man, stripped to the waist, working on a vegetable plot to the right. It took another moment to realise that the man was Tory. She hesitated, but he'd already seen her.

She watched him rise slowly, lay down his tools and walk towards her. His movements looked fluid and languid, in direct contrast to her own inner turmoil.

"Now, here's a surprise! Mrs Griffiths, if I'm not mistaken."

His skin was brown, his hands dark with soil, his hair a shade fairer than when he'd come to the wedding. Clearly he was used to working outside. She tried not to look at his naked torso.

He must have noted her discomfort, because he crossed to the seating area, lifted a shirt from the back of a bench and pulled it on. Ruth looked away. She could no longer remember why she'd come.

"This is quite a place!" she said, neutrally.

"Thanks. It works for us."

"Us?"

"The group."

"You're a commune?"

Tory shrugged. "If you want to call it that. It's just a different way of living. Pool resources, live more simply, more creatively."

"Blimey, and there was me thinking you'd have got more establishment in your old age!" Ruth pushed her fists in the pockets of her suit jacket.

"Sorry, I should get you a drink," said Tory, though he made no move to do so.

"No, don't worry. It's just a flying visit. I happened to be passing."

He nodded, but didn't look like he believed her. "Quite a surprise. Not that you're not welcome, of course."

"I needed to ask you something. About the night of the wedding." She took a breath. "Did you leave us your lottery ticket?"

He gave her an amused glance. "It might surprise you to know I don't do the lottery!"

"The favours - the little gold envelopes?"

"Ah."

The door closest to them appeared to lead into a narrow store or pantry. Tory leaned in around it, and lifted something down from a hook on the back. Ruth recognised it as the linen jacket he'd worn to the wedding.

He began going through the pockets, and finally withdrew a small gold envelope. "Like this you mean?" He tossed it across to her. It was still sealed. And it was definitely his name on the little handmade label.

"You didn't even check it?" She was astounded.

He shrugged. "I'm not interested in money. You know that."

"Yes, but..." She paused. "It's one thing to say that. I mean, I wouldn't expect you to actually go out and buy a ticket, but when someone gives you one, not to be curious...well, it's perverse."

Tory laughed, deep and resonant. "And that behaviour surprises you?"

She tipped her head to concede the point.

"Look, what are the chances of winning? Infinitesimal! I just never gave it a thought. It's no big deal."

"And you're still not curious?"

"Nope."

"You might have won enough money to keep your commune going for ever."

"But that's the point. In order to work effectively, the group has to keep itself, fund itself, through its own endeavours. It's not a holiday camp. We get by. We don't need the money. It would actually be detrimental."

Ruth shook her head in disbelief, and held the little gold envelope out to him. He didn't take it.

"You open it if it bothers you so much."

"It doesn't bother me."

"Well, that's ok then."

There was a fire pit by the seating area, smouldering gently.

"Just chuck it in there then," said Tory.

"Then you'll never know."

"I don't want to know." He grinned at her. "Why did you want to know about my ticket, anyway? Someone left one and you thought it was me?"

Ruth nodded. "Five numbers and the bonus ball." She stared at the gold envelope. She'd been so certain.

"And now you know it wasn't me?"

Ruth shrugged.

"You can't think who it was?"

"No...I can't."

"Was the ticket still in the envelope?"

She nodded.

"Was it sealed?"

She tried to remember. Had she had to open it?

"I have an idea." Tory nodded at the gold envelope in her hands. "Why don't you take that with you, and give it to the person who donated theirs. Seems fair doesn't it?"

"But that's the point! I don't know who that was!"

"Really?" Tory was grinning at her. "Can't you guess?"

She shook her head, furious. It came to her at once that she was indeed over him. Absolutely and completely. She felt cut adrift. A helium balloon in the sky.

"Have you got a pen?" asked Tory.

Ruth fished in her bag and found an old biro.

Tory took the golden envelope and the pen, peeled off his label, and wrote a name in its place.

"There we go. Deliver that - with my love, if you would."

"He never even spoke to me at the wedding."

Lizzy sat on the bench, with her hands in her lap, not touching the gold envelope.

"He said you blanked him every time he tried. Said it was the only reason he'd agreed to come in the first place, and he was completely miserable all evening - that's why he left early." Ruth remembered the conversation outside the toilets, and blushed at her own ego. When he'd spoken of happiness, she'd assumed he'd been talking about her. Later, when Tory was staring at the three of them, she'd assumed she was the object of his gaze. She felt hot with shame every time she thought of it.

"It's funny," said Lizzy, "you and Tory might not have got together at all if it hadn't been for that timetable clash. We ended up swapping groups for that tutorial - do you remember?"

Ruth shook her head.

"If they'd kept the original groups, I'd have been in Tory's tutorial." Lizzy gave a rueful smile. "Life is always just luck."

They looked out across the park in silence. Lizzy hadn't wanted to meet at her flat, or Ruth's home. She was furious that Ruth had gone back on her word. Ruth wasn't yet sure if she'd been forgiven.

"When you gave us the ticket," asked Ruth, "did you know?"

"That it was a winning ticket?" Lizzy made a face. "Nope. I gave it to you because you'd had to give up your ticket because of your Aunt Mags. I felt sorry for you and Phil, so I gave you mine - it was meant to be a bit of a joke. And then of course, you said it was a winner. I couldn't very well say it was me without making it look like I was looking for gratitude - or worse, a share."

"But you ought to have a share!" said Ruth quickly. "Phil and I have spoken about it - we've agreed."

Lizzy shook her head. "No, I gave it to you in good faith. You can't ask for a bit of a gift back just because it turns out to be valuable. Besides, I've got my own ticket now." She picked up the gold envelope and ran her thumb over her name, written in Tory's looping handwriting. "And this one's better because of the sentiments which come with it."

"You'll go and see him now?"

"Yes, of course. I just - it's a lot to take in, you know? After so long. The relief...it's like falling from a great height. Feel a bit sick."

"Like vertigo."

Lizzy nodded. "Exactly like." She paused. "And you're ok?"

"I've done what I wanted - got him out of my system, if that's what you mean." Ruth blew out her cheeks. "I asked him why you two had never got to together at uni. He said, 'Because, Ruth, darling - you were always in the way.' "

Lizzy winced.

"But it's true," said Ruth. "I feel such an idiot. All these years, in my head it was him playing dog-in-the-manger with me. In reality it was the other way around. I just couldn't see it."

Lizzy said nothing. Ruth felt the sting of her silence, but couldn't blame her. Lizzy had always been there for her - supportive and true. She should have guessed straight away that the lottery ticket had been Lizzy's, but even after seeing Tory, she'd needed proof. She'd gone straight home and told Phil everything - then they'd phoned Maddie. Mads had been evasive at first, but soon admitted she'd seen Lizzy slip the envelope in with the other cards. Now it was impossible to imagine any other truth.

"You know you've changed my life - mine and Phil's - with that ticket." Ruth looked at her. "We'll always owe you for that."

"You've changed mine with this one." Lizzy held up the envelope. "So we're quits."

"Are you going to open it?" said Ruth.

Lizzy shrugged. "Maybe."

"I mean, I know the numbers - if you wanted to check. You've probably not got that long left to claim if you've won anything. There's a time limit."

"Maybe when I go and see Tory. Maybe not."

Ruth felt a surge of irritation. She and Tory were going to be a perfect match.

And then the feeling vanished. She leant over, gave Lizzy a hug, and got up from the bench.

"Good luck."

"Thanks." Lizzy smiled at her. "You too."

Ruth walked back across the park to the car. She climbed in the passenger side and looked across at Phil.

"Mission accomplished?" he asked

She nodded.

"Is Liz going to be alright?"

They watched her for a moment, sitting alone on the bench.

"Yes, I think so."

Phil leaned across and kissed her. "Home, then?"

She smiled and nodded. "Yes, please."

She took one last glance at the figure on the bench as they drove away. She was beyond lucky to have had a friend as good as Lizzy.

THE ONE BEFORE

It's strange putting my key in the lock. I feel as if I should lift the heavy knocker and wait, but of course there's no-one here to answer.

The door resists when I try to open it, and I have to squat and reach around to push a mountain of post out of the way. This in itself brings a new stab of guilt. It's not been that long since my last visit, surely? When I get inside, I realise it's mostly junk mail and the local free paper. I gather everything into a pile, and go down the hall to the kitchen to sort through it on the table. The only things of any importance are a gas bill and a square, handwritten envelope which feels like a greetings card. The rest goes straight in the box under the sink where mum keeps all the recycling.

When I straighten, I am momentarily distracted by mum's garden. The daffs are just starting to flower, and there is fresh green growth everywhere. I wish I could bring her to look, but the doctors have advised that bringing her back home even for a visit will simply confuse her all the more. I have to bite my tongue when given advice like this; she is far beyond confused. Still, it's sad that she won't see her beloved garden awakening from its winter sleep.

My phone pings. A message from work. I need to be back for a meeting at 3pm. There's no time to stand, gazing out of windows.

I head upstairs, pushing open the door to mum's bedroom. The air inside is stuffy, a mix of stale air and her favourite perfume. I throw open a window and hear birds, the distant buzz of traffic, and somewhere a premature lawn mower. Opening the wardrobe makes me feel vaguely uncomfortable - I would never have touched her things if she was here - but she needs some more clothes now the weather is getting warmer. I select a few blouses and tops, a couple of skirts, a pretty dress which was always a favourite. She'll need some shoes too. I crouch at the bottom of the wardrobe. All her footwear is stored neatly in the original boxes. She has smaller feet than me; the shoes look dainty and beautifully kept. She isn't the sort to kick them off the minute she gets in the door like I do. She likes colour and detail. Heels and bows. The sort of stuff that it isn't possible to wear in real life.

A sigh escapes me. My mother is no longer part of real life.

At the very back of the wardrobe is a final shoe box. I stretch out my fingertips and pull it towards me. It's heavy in comparison with the others, and when I flip off the lid, I realise why. It contains not a pair of shoes, but a stack of old paper memories. There are clumsy birthday cards I made as a child, garish paint, browning glue and fragments of remaining glitter. Valentine's cards from Dad - always the romantic, right until the end. Letters from mum's long-dead sister, Christine. Postcards from student-me from various far-flung corners of the world. Right at the bottom, there is a bundle of papers folded into a small carrier bag.

I half-think to put everything back. It's not my place to pry. This is not what I came here for. Time is ticking away. I need to get the clothes and shoes over to my mum, and then get back to work. But I hold the bundle in my lap, stare at the patterned carpet that I've always hated, and my eyes mist with tears.

I miss her so much. And that's the hardest thing. Missing her when she's still with us.

I rub my eyes, and unfold the bundle from the bag.

Inside there are more letters and cards, in an unfamiliar hand. The paper is foxed and the folds fragile, and where the post marks are still legible, I realise I'm looking at correspondence from way back. An old boyfriend of mum's before dad! How odd. I never remember her mentioning an old flame - but he must have been important to her if she kept his letters all this time.

I open a final envelope, slide out a folded document and, as I do so, a photo drops out. A black and white wedding photo. And then I feel all the breath knocked out of me. The bride is mum. She's very young; just a teenager I'd guess. But her face is radiant with joy, staring up at the man standing next to her. He in turn is gazing down at her, his expression full of love and delight.

I unfold the document. The marriage certificate confirms that my guess is correct. My mother married Joseph William Carter a week after her 18th birthday.

I stare at Joseph Carter. A man my mum clearly adored and yet of whom I knew nothing until this moment. He has bright twinkling eyes, a shock of blonde hair, and a ready grin.

"Wow, mum," I say out loud. "He's quite a catch."

I know mum was 27 when she married Dad. She always joked that it was because he took so long to ask. He in turn always maintained that he was afraid to ask before as he knew she'd turn him down. Now there's some context for both arguments.

When I try to slide the marriage certificate and the photo back into the envelope, there's something in the way. I pull out another document. A death certificate. I stare at the date. Joseph died three months after the wedding. Killed in a motorcycle accident.

My poor mum. I stare at the wedding photo again; two young people blissfully unaware of the tragedy just around the corner.

My phone starts buzzing in my handbag. I let the call go to answerphone. I'm going to be late for work, but I don't care.

Mum is in the "Lavender" room. They are big on engaging all the senses here. The home is full of interesting sounds, scents, colours, textures, and lighting. I'm not sure it makes any difference, but it at least feels plausible.

She is sat at a table, concentrating on something. The pose is striking simply because these days she cannot concentrate on anything. I step a little closer, and see she is painting small yellow flowers onto a piece of A4 paper. She has a fine paintbrush and a squat pot of squidgy looking paint. When I get closer still, I see there are faint lines for her to follow.

I slide into the seat across from her and smile brightly. "You're making a lovely job of that."

Mum looks up. "Oh, thank you." She glances off to her left for a moment, and then back at me, leaning forward conspiratorially. "It's for my daughter's homework. She's supposed to hand it in tomorrow, but she won't do it. Not interested in art. Not a bit. But I don't want her to lose marks. School is so important."

"Absolutely." I try to think of a time my mum ever did any of my homework on my behalf. It simply never would have happened. She would have regarded it as cheating.

"So, what does she like if she doesn't like art?" I ask.

"Oh, music - that's her passion."

"Really?" I can't keep the surprise out of my voice. I like listening to music as much as the next person, but I've never showed any interest in learning about it.

"The guitar mostly."

I grin. "Wow! I didn't know that."

"She gets it from her father. He was incredible on the guitar."

My grin fades a little. It might all be nonsense, of course. Mostly her conversations are these days. But maybe, just maybe, she's not talking about my dad (who certainly never played the guitar to my knowledge). Maybe she's talking about Joseph. I think of the man in the photo. He looks like the kind of guy who would have played guitar.

A thought flits into my mind: perhaps mum had a baby before me? Another daughter, 10 years my senior, who has been leading a parallel life somewhere? But mum would never have given up a baby, surely?

I gaze at her, a thousand questions queuing up in my mind. But of course, even if I were to ask them, mum doesn't really know the answers any more.

As if to confirm this, she says suddenly, "Do you have children?"

"No, I don't." I smile gently. "Never married."

"That doesn't seem to make any difference these days!" she says, dipping her paintbrush into a jar of water and swirling it around.

"Never met the right guy!" I say flippantly, the same lie I trot out every time.

"That's a shame, my dear," she says. "I was very lucky."

I wait for her to add something more, but she doesn't. She wipes the paintbrush carefully on a piece of kitchen towel.

"Would you pop that by the radiator to dry?" she asks.

And I take the paper and put it on the table close to the heat. My phone buzzes again.

She looks enquiringly at me.

"I'd better go. It's work. I'm supposed to be in a meeting."

"Oh absolutely," she says, "wouldn't want you to get in trouble."

I get to my feet, then reach into my bag and pull out

the photograph. "I just wanted to give you this."

She takes the photo and a look of amazement passes over her face. It is as if she has been lit up from within. She gazes at it with absolutely joy. "Oh, my word!"

I don't wait to find out what the word is. She doesn't even notice as I slip from the room, and run out to the car. I keep the image of her expression fresh in my mind as I drive.

For a few seconds, I saw my mum again.

THE BUSY BEE

Heat rose up from the paving slabs, baking the soles of Leah's bare feet. Even in her lightest cotton dress, she felt too hot, the backs of her knees prickling uncomfortably. She squinted up at the sky, huge and blue, the sun glaring, and wondered how her mother could still find the energy to weed the borders. Mrs Blake was on her knees by the herb garden, attacking some particularly tenacious couch grass.

A welcome breeze ruffled the fabric of Leah's dress, and sent the lavender heads bobbing. Insects buzzed and darted, before resettling on the flower heads. A bee with unusual markings caught her eye. It was smaller than the others, its tiny body looking almost fury.

"Mum, what's this bee?" Leah called across the garden.

"What darling?" Mrs Blake half lifted her head, pausing to carefully remove a stinging nettle from her fork with a gloved hand.

"This bee, it's different from the others. What is it?"

Leah saw her mum push herself reluctantly to her feet and come to look.

"I don't know, sweetheart," said Mrs Blake, gazing at the bee. "It's a rather lovely little thing. I think they like the lavender – and the Michaelmas daisies." She turned to go back to her weeding. "Why don't you have a look in the encyclopaedia?"

Leah hopped and skipped up the back step and plunged into the darkness of the house, blinking as her eyes adjusted. The encyclopaedia was kept on a shelf in the hall, a monstrously heavy tome with thick textured covers. She flicked through the pages to bees and then honeybees but the only pictures were of the fat bumble bees she was used to seeing in the garden, and there were no descriptions that matched the little bee she'd seen.

When Monday came and her mother went into town to do the grocery shopping, Leah went with her, but slipped off to the library in search of bee books. There wasn't much of interest on the shelves, but Mrs McKenzie behind the desk said she would check with the other local libraries and order anything which looked useful. When Leah went back the following week, there were three books waiting for her. A practical guide to bee keeping, something about the role of bees in pollination and farming which looked very dull, and a very simple spotters guide. In the latter, Leah found her bee on page 34. She went home, triumphant.

When school started back, Leah chose bees as the topic of her autumn term project, and her teachers were startled by her dedication and growing knowledge in the area. They put her forward for a special residential course for particularly able pupils in science. Practically fainting with shyness, Leah was dropped off at an imposing Georgian building – once some grand family pile, now an education centre – and spent a week with other gifted children working on various science and environmental projects. Over the days, her shyness evaporated, and when her mum came to pick her up on the last day, Leah found she was sad to be leaving.

While other mums complained their children didn't study enough, Mrs Blake began to worry that Leah was working too hard. She always seemed to be locked away in her bedroom, textbooks piled high on her desk, the floor littered with scribbled notes. But the work paid off, and Leah sailed through her exams, before heading off to university.

In her little room in the halls of residence, Leah lined up the books on her new reading list. She recognised one. It was an updated edition of that dull looking book on pollination and farming. Now it didn't look quite so dull.

The lecturers were as pleased with her dedication and progress as her teachers had been, and owing to her exceptional knowledge, she was invited to attend a conference in London on work to reverse the trend of falling bee populations. After the first presentation, a young man stood up to ask a question, and as he sat back down, caught Leah staring at him. He held her gaze, and then smiled in a way which made her stomach flip over.

In the coffee break, the young man introduced himself as Seamus, a postgrad, now eager to bring to everyone's attention the plight of the bees.

"Join me on the next campaign?" said Seamus, deep brown eyes as rich as chocolate, and a voice like velvet. "It'd be grand."

For a while, Leah teetered on the edge of love, before falling in.

They wrote well-informed letters to influential people, protested at sites where habitats were being destroyed. They appeared on local radio programmes, wrote articles for newspapers and magazines. They were constantly on the move.

"Darling, are you sure you're not doing too much?" said Mrs Blake in one of their increasingly brief telephone calls.

Leah, hopping from one foot to another, watched Seamus out of the corner of her eye, successfully flagging down a van for a lift. "I'm fine, mum, honestly. Gotta go. Love you."

But while she didn't want to admit it, Leah was beginning to find the peripatetic lifestyle draining. She wanted more time with Seamus, just the two of them. And she wanted Seamus to want it too.

She applied for and was offered a university lectureship, which came with a cramped, utilitarian flat on the edge of the campus. Relieved to be able to put down roots at last, shallow though they may have been, she hoped Seamus might settle down with her. But he proved thoroughly rootless. He would turn up at the flat periodically, with a bin liner full of washing, beg a bath and a hot meal, recount his latest crusade on behalf of the bees and, if she was lucky, stay a day or two, a sensual being in her bed, a bright flash of intellect in their shared conversations. But then he would be gone, off to the next campaign, and the flat would feel hollow and silent. She would put the radio on, pick up the unread papers and try to read.

When she wasn't teaching, she worked on a definitive book on falling bee populations and their effect on food production and the wider economy. It was published, and put on the reading lists of a number of university courses. It did better than expected. Her publishers invited her to write more, allowing her to go part-time at the university.

The flat seemed more hollow and silent than ever. She fancied Seamus's visits were more sporadic now. When he did turn up, muddy boots kicked off on the doormat, a grubby coat slung over the back of the sofa, she hardly recognised the man who trawled through her fridge to make a sandwich, pausing only to peck her on the cheek. The chocolate eyes were looking a little bloodshot these days, and if he made it as far as her bed, it was usually only to fall into a deep sleep.

A dark shadow fell across Leah's life when, quite suddenly after a short illness, Mrs Blake died. Leah found herself the beneficiary of a reasonable amount of money she didn't really know what to do with. She would have happily given it back in order to have a bit more time with her mum, but that wasn't an option. She thought of the old house where she'd been brought up. It had been sold years ago, her mother unable to keep up with the garden, and unwilling to let it get out of hand or watch someone else do it for her.

Leah told Seamus she was thinking of buying a house. A house with a garden. Seamus looked at her as though she was talking nonsense. "What would you want to be doing that for?" he said, tucking into the last of her casserole. "You don't even like gardening!"

Leah's courage failed her. She didn't mention that when she thought of a garden, she thought of Seamus and herself together in it. Maybe a swing or a climbing frame for the children. The dream seemed fuzzy and distant.

When she woke the next morning, Seamus had gone. There was a brief scribbled note on the kitchen table saying he'd had to go early and had not wanted to disturb her. She stood for a long while with the kiss-less note in her hand, then she screwed it up and threw it in the recycling bin.

The house turned out to be nothing like the one she'd been brought up in, but it felt right the moment she walked across the threshold. The garden was huge, and had evidently been too much for the previous owners. Leah would need a gardener. Some friends of friends suggested someone. His name was Eddie. He'd been in middle management, but widowed early in life, he'd decided to give up the rat race and become a gardener. He sounded promising.

He arrived two minutes early, and Leah offered him a cuppa. He smiled bashfully, hardly daring to look her in the eye, and when he took the mug, she noticed his hands shook very slightly. But he seemed not a bit put off by the size of the garden. She saw his eyes running over the choking weeds and brambles, the faded blooms of half hidden roses, and she knew he was the one.

"I'll have it right for you in no time," he said. "Could start tomorrow if you like."

She did like.

She turned the old dining room at the back of the house into a study, its large French windows overlooking the garden. Looking up from her work, she would see Eddie, strimming back the weeds, uncovering forgotten paths, resurrecting borders. She liked the slow methodical way that he worked, the long hours he put in. She liked that he was always there, a comforting presence.

One morning, he turned up towing a trailer behind his van.

"Got something for you," he said, taking her hand and leading her out to the driveway. His grip was warm and strong, his palms calloused. It should have felt strange that he was holding her hand, but it didn't. When they reached the trailer and he let go, she wished he hadn't.

In the trailer was a rough wooden garden bench.

"I was on another job, and they told me to burn it." Eddie ran his hand over the wood, like a caress. "Seemed a waste, so I asked if I could have it. I thought it would be just the thing for that back wall where you get the sun in the evenings."

Leah beamed at him. She didn't often get presents. "It's perfect, thank you." And unable to resist, she reached up and kissed his tanned cheek.

Eddie blushed all the way to his ears.

She helped him heft the bench off the trailer and carry it round the back of the house. He was right of course – it was perfect by the suntrap wall. The garden was looking lived in at last. Leah felt a thrill of delight run through her.

From the house, she heard the shrill sound of the phone ringing. She made a face at Eddie and went in to answer it.

The faded velvet voice was Seamus. Leah was startled to realise she'd almost blotted out his existence. The line was poor; she could barely make out what he was saying. She gathered he wanted to 'drop by' that evening.

With the receiver pressed to her ear, she gazed through the French windows at Eddie. He was putting a new lavender bush in one of the borders, his strong hands firming up the earth around the roots. He looked up, and caught her eye. Blue, his eyes, blue like a tumbling waterfall. Clear and pure and bright.

Leah heard herself say, "Sorry Seamus, it's not convenient. I don't think I can do this anymore."

She put the phone down, and went out into the garden. Together, she and Eddie stood by the lavender bush and watched a bee land on one of the flower heads.

"Hello Mr Bumble," said Eddie.

Leah was about to correct him; the body shape and markings were clearly not those of a bumble bee. But she held her tongue. What did it matter? They were standing in a beautiful garden. The sun was dappling through the trees. A gentle breeze was nudging the flowers.

She looked up at Eddie, his shoulders broad from all that digging, his expression one of pure contentment.

"Take a break for a few minutes," said Leah, "Let's just sit on the bench and admire your garden."

"Your garden," Eddie corrected.

Leah shook her head and smiled. "Our garden then."

Eddie looked at her, his waterfall eyes tumbling. "I'd like that very much."

ABOUT THE STORIES

Symptoms - Originally published in Woman's Weekly in July 2018.

Forgetting - Originally published by now defunct website 'Readwave.com'. The site was a good idea for sharing stories and getting feedback, so it's a shame it didn't last. On the upside, I had to clean our fridge so that I could take a photo of the teapot standing in it as an illustration for the website. This prompted my husband to ask if I could write a story about an oven...

Resolution - Placed 4th in the Erewash Writers' Open Short Story competition in November 2016. I find titles really difficult, so I was a tiny bit smug that 'Resolution' worked on several levels for this story.

Party Pooper - Originally published in Woman's Weekly in June 2017.

All in the Cards - Inspired by a real pack of cards given to me by my mum years ago as a joke stocking filler. As a would-be writer herself, I hope she would have been chuffed that her gift sparked a story idea.

The Middle Drawer - My modern take on the original Bluebeard folktale. In the original, of course, the heroine discovers the bloody corpses of her husband's previous wives. In my version, what the heroine discovers in the locked room is that her husband is a fraud - thereby effectively killing her love, respect and admiration for him.

Raspberry Ripple - Originally published by the lovely website FictiveDream.com in November 2016. (Just for the record, whilst raspberry ripple is indeed delicious, my favourite ice cream is rum & raison, but I don't think you can go far wrong with traditional vanilla either.)

Going Solo - Originally published by The People's Friend in September 2013.

Skin Deep - Written originally as a piece for my (continually supportive) writers' group after a Spa day with friends got me thinking about what it must be like for the girls that work there.

Luck of the Draw - If you have bucket loads of personal integrity and have never done anything you're ashamed of, or you've never misinterpreted a situation because you saw it only from your own hugely egotistical view, then I salute you (enviously). For the rest of us mere mortals, I wanted to write a story where the heroine wasn't actually that nice, and treated others poorly just because she was seeing a situation only from her own very limited perspective.

The One Before - The lives lived by your loved-ones before you came along are always intriguing - there's so much you can never really know, particularly where the older generation is concerned. It's all too easy to forget that the elderly were not always so, that not so long ago, they too were young - full of the same energies and impulses, the same hopes and dreams. With Alzheimer's and dementia even the memories of these are lost, which becomes even more intriguing, and desperately sad.

The Busy Bee - Originally published by The People's Friend in August 2013.

Bonus story, from the collection:
The Camel in the Garden

FIVE PER CENT

Josh stands with his hands on his hips, bony elbows jutting out, and frowns into the mirror.

'I don't look like a bee. I look like a fat boy in a stripy jumper.'

In any other circumstance, I might feel the urge to giggle but, right this second, it doesn't seem a joking matter. Josh's frank assessment of my costume-making abilities is a low blow.

'You don't look fat – you look nice and round like a bee should.'

This is a bit of a lie. The stuffing I've shoved under the stripy jumper is uneven and lumpy. He looks like a bee with mumps.

'And these are girls trousers,' says Josh.

'They don't tend to do leggings for boys,' I say. My smile in the mirror looks forced.

'And the wings aren't right. They're butterfly wings, not bee wings.'

'They didn't have bee wings in the shop,' I say, giving the gauzy fabric a tweak. 'It was the best I could do.'

'George's mum is making his costume and it looks brilliant,' says Josh folding his arms across his chest. The gesture makes him look so much like Craig, I feel a stabbing pain in the core of me.

'In that case, George's mum is very clever,' I say, 'But I expect she has a bit more time than I do because she doesn't have to go to work.'

'You didn't use to.'

'I did. I've always worked.'

'Not all the time,' says Josh.

'You mean not full time.'

Josh ignores the correction. 'You'd have made my costume before.'

Before.

In the mirror, my reflection chews its lip. Josh is quite right. Two years ago, maybe even 18 months ago, I'd have been busy for several evenings with my needle and thread, looking through old pattern books of my mum's, picking out just the right fabric from my stash of off-cuts. Craig would have looked on, amused at my ingenuity, envious of my energy. A year ago, mum would have made the costume on my behalf – knowing it was another of the thousand and one jobs I couldn't bring myself to do.

'Yes, darling, I would have,' I say. I kneel, put my arm around his slender waist, under the imperfect wings, and try to hug him. His body is stiff and unyielding. 'I'm sorry I didn't have time.'

'You would have had time if...' Josh's defiant voice wavers. He can't finish the sentence, but he doesn't have to.

'I had to go to the launch. It's part of my work.'

'It was a party. You went to a party. People don't go to parties for work. They go to an office, or a factory.'

Is it worth arguing? Do I have to try to convince my son, in the same way as I did my parents all those years ago, that PR is a job – that hosting events with canapés and champagne counts as a worthwhile occupation?

I let my arm drop. 'It was one evening, Josh. One evening, that's all.'

I push myself to my feet, and go to the door. Out of

the corner of my eye I see Josh tugging the stripy jumper over his head, crushing the wings.

'We need you for London.' Marc tosses a thick envelope onto my desk. 'Overnighter. Man the trade stand at the show. Dinner and drinks in the evening.'

I goggle. 'I can't – not overnight. I could do the trade stand – as long as I could get back –'

Marc shakes his head. 'Nope. Got to be our rep at the dinner. No-one else is free and we can't be seen not to have someone there. Could put us in a very vulnerable position.'

'But I can't leave Josh overnight.'

Marc, half way to the door, stops and frowns. 'Your mum can have him, can't she? Just for one night?'

'Yes, but –'

'I mean, come on, you must have left him before.'

Once.

I press my palms against the cold granite either side of the wash basin. My wedding ring, loose on my finger, clinks against the hard surface.

When Craig's condition suddenly nosedived on that April afternoon, mum managed to collect Josh from our house before the ambulance arrived. She'd made it sound like an adventure. Throwing a few things in a bag for him, bustling him out of the house with just a squeeze of my arm to say all the unsayable stuff. Good luck. Hope this isn't it. Call me when you know.

So yes. I left him before. For one night. When his father died.

I lift my head, look at myself in the mirror. In my ultra-fashionable suit, my over-sculpted costume jewellery, I am a PR executive. Where has Josh's mum gone? Does Josh wonder the same thing?

A plump woman stands closest to the school gates,

ineffectually pulling a shapeless cardigan over her rump. She's not quite brave enough to join the other mums, who stand in a huddle, smiling and comfortable, smelling of washing powder and carrying capacious bags which no doubt hold essentials like plasters and tissues and antiseptic cream. Two hard, wiry women with gold hooped earrings and tight little tops stand nearby. One is smoking, which is forbidden – less by law than by the accepted protocols of the other mums.

I keep a little way off. Too posh for the smokers and the cardigan. Too something else for the proper mummies. I feel their eyes on me every so often, appraising, spotting the holes in my disguise. The forgotten-hairdresser's-appointment. The creased skirt. The chipped nail varnish. The bits where Josh's mum shows through the PR executive exterior.

There is no bell, but without warning, the double doors of the nearest building are pushed open, and there is a tumble of bodies and school bags, pushed up sleeves and skew-whiff ties. They resolve themselves into individuals and there is Josh, small and determined, eyes fixed on me.

I force a smile. My rehearsed speech sticks in my throat.

We are at mum's. The smell of roasting chicken wafts comfortingly from the kitchen. A mug of tea in my hand, I gaze through the patio windows at Josh in the garden. He is intent on some complicated game involving periodic whizzing around the lawn at speed, and then coming back to 'base' at the rockery.

'He's angry with me,' I say.

'He's not angry with you,' says Mum 'he's angry with the world.'

I shake my head. 'I need to be home for him more. The job – it's not working out.'

I put my mug down on the dining table. The wall ahead of me is a patchwork of photographs: me on my first bike;

me in my school uniform, glowering at the camera; me at my graduation, almost sophisticated. A group of us from my gap year, travelling – tanned and dusty – Craig just another guy. Craig and me on our wedding day, smiling Hollywood smiles. Me pregnant and grinning, with Craig's hand on my swollen stomach.

Where have all those versions of me gone? I almost don't recognise myself.

Mum says, 'You're not expected to be perfect, you know. You can't do it all.'

I smile ruefully. 'It's just that he's the most important thing. Being his mum is the most important thing – I hate not being able to do it a hundred per cent.'

Mum frowns. 'You can't be a mum a hundred per cent. You've got to keep a bit back for you. Even if it's only five per cent.'

I gaze at the photographs. What would five per cent look like?

I keep my plastic smile in place as more people walk past the stand. They glance briefly at the hoarding behind me, barely taking it in. I could get out from behind the trestle table, where our literature is splayed in an untouched fan, and talk to punters, but the conference is drawing to a close. People are drifting away, wondering if they can fit in a quick look round the shops, or a pint in the bar.

I rock onto the balls of my feet, itching to move. My watch says 3.56pm. Mum will have collected Josh by now. Should I call?

A guy with a branded lanyard round his neck and a clipboard pauses across the aisle from me, and gives me an overfamiliar wave as though we're best mates. He may be the same guy who showed me to my pitch, but I can't swear to it.

'We're all meeting at the bar at six,' he calls over, holding up all the digits of one hand and the thumb of the other.

In that instance, my decision is made. I'll cancel the hotel on my way.

I shake my head, trying to inject as much regret as possible into my expression. 'Can't make it – got a bit of an emergency at home – have to go, I'm afraid.'

He makes a crestfallen face, like a miming clown.

When he's gone, I sweep the promotional guff off the table and into a box. The hoarding is on a spring and rolls into a tube. The whole lot is safely piled into my trolley in eight minutes, and I'm off to the railway station.

Marc blows a non-existent fringe off his forehead. He won't look me in the eye.

'I'm not saying you're not pulling your weight.' His lips purse, as though he's trying to think of a way to phrase it. 'But it comes with the territory – the travel, the time away from home. You knew all that when you came back.'

Yes, but I was desperate.

Yes, but I needed the money.

Yes, but I thought I could make it work.

'And you knew I was a one parent family.' The minute I say it, I want to take it back. It sounds like I'm asking for pity.

'I was happy to have you back because you were great at your job.'

I note the past tense.

'Perhaps,' Marc adds, 'neither of us had really thought through the implications of the change in your personal circumstances.'

I stand up quickly. My chair glides back on its casters. I pull my handbag from the desk drawer.

'What are you doing?' asks Marc.

I look him square in the face. 'Letting you off the hook.'

'Moving where?' asks Josh. His expression lies somewhere between suspicion and avid interest.

'Somewhere smaller.'

'Will I still have my own room?'

I laugh. 'Of course.'

He looks around at the house which has been his home always. 'I like it here though.'

'Which would you prefer,' I say, 'this house, and me working all the time, or a smaller place and me only working some of the time?'

'This house and you in it always.'

I make a face.

'*Okay!*' he says, like the characters in the programmes he watches on telly. 'Smaller house and you home more.'

'Good,' I say, 'me too.' I pat the seat next to me on the sofa and he flumps down beside me making the cushions bounce. The screen of my laptop shows a page of houses for sale. 'Come and look at these and tell me which you like.'

They are all cramped and nondescript, but if it would buy me more time with my son, I would love any one of them.

They're a nice couple. She smiles a lot. Glances at him each time she sees something else about the house she likes. When I see him absently catch hold of her little finger to lead her to the window, I feel a pang.

I do all the right things – offer them coffee, give them space to explore alone. I've 'de-cluttered' so already the house feels sparse and impersonal.

Josh hangs over the bannister desperate for them to come up so he can show off his room, which now looks like something out of an interiors magazine – the perfect child's bedroom.

The husband says, 'And can I ask why you're moving?'

'We're downsizing.'

'So mummy can go half-time,' calls Josh from the bannister.

I smile. 'Part-time.'

'Good for you,' says the wife.

'And have you found somewhere to move to?' says the husband.

I think of the three places Josh and I have seen which fall into our miserly price range. A ground floor flat (very cheap, but communal garden horrid – a clear no), an uninspiring 1970s semi (spacious, but dull) and a Victorian two bed terrace in need of a major revamp. My head said take the semi, but Josh clamoured for the terrace, and my heart was delighted to agree.

'Yes, and the place we're interested in is currently empty, so no chain.'

The couple glance at one another. I know they think it's perfect. Just as Craig and I did when we moved in.

I have to admire whichever member of staff has written the school play. It's certainly ambitious for primary. There are kids dressed as flowers, or trees, as farmers and shop keepers and scientists, some in suits representing Big Business. And there is Josh – in his bee costume. It is slightly improved. Better stuffing for the jumper gives him a more even, bee-like body. And I've managed to make the wings less butterfly-like. And he even has antenna. When he buzzes onto the stage, there is a group 'Ahh!' from the audience.

In the story, Humble Bumble is sad because he thinks he's just a tiny insignificant bee. Then a wise old owl (George – Josh was right, his costume is amazing) shows him the part bees play in the whole ecosystem, and Humble Bumble realises he's just as important as the mighty oak and the rich businessmen.

I'm not convinced that the kids fully grasp the meaning of the play, but after the fall of the curtain, and two lots of theatrical bowing, Josh rushes out to greet me and Mum, still buzzing in every sense of the word.

I sweep him up in my arms and Mum gets out her camera, snapping us in mid hug. She shows us the image on the screen – Josh, still dressed as a bee, beaming; me, in jeans and my favourite blouse, looking every inch Josh's mum. Well, maybe not every inch. Five per cent is me. You might not be able to see it in the photo, but I know it's there.

ABOUT THE AUTHOR

Jenny Roman had her first short story published in PONY magazine when she was a teenager, and has since written short stories and articles for a variety of magazines including Woman's Weekly, Writers' Forum, Countryside Tales, Debut, Scribble, The People's Friend, The Weekly News, and Yours.

Jenny has an MA in Creative Writing from Nottingham Trent University, has had stories short-listed or placed in a host of writing competitions and has herself been a story competition judge.

She is a member of a Writers' Group and strongly recommends this to anyone thinking of writing creatively. When she's not writing, you'll probably find her either in the garden, off walking the dogs, or mucking out the horses!

To find out more about Jenny and her books, visit: www.jennyroman.wordpress.com.

Keep up to date with news and special offers (and claim an exclusive free ebook) by signing up for her (rather sporadic) newsletter at:
bit.ly/JennyRomanNewsletter

And finally, word-of-mouth is crucial for any author to succeed. If you enjoyed these stories, please leave a review on Amazon or Goodreads, or simply tell a friend.

Thank you!